The Road to Atlantis

The Road to Atlantis

a novel

Leo Brent Robillard

TURNSTONE PRESS

The Road to Atlantis
copyright © Leo Brent Robillard 2015

Turnstone Press
Artspace Building
206-100 Arthur Street
Winnipeg, MB
R3B 1H3 Canada
www.TurnstonePress.com

Turnstone Press gratefully acknowledges the assistance of the Canada
Council for the Arts, the Manitoba Arts Council, the Government of
Canada through the Canada Book Fund, and the Province of Manitoba
through the Book Publishing Tax Credit and the Book Publisher
Marketing Assistance Program.

Printed and bound in Canada by Friesens for Turnstone Press.

Library and Archives Canada Cataloguing in Publication

Robillard, Leo Brent, 1973–, author

   The road to Atlantis / Leo Brent Robillard.

ISBN 978-0-88801-555-6 (pbk.)

   I. Title.

PS8635.O237R63 2015   C813'.6   C2015-903093-5

For my mother and in loving memory of my father.

The Road to Atlantis

Cape May

David lay in the sun. He felt the warm rays on his back. His swimsuit was almost dry. It was made from some sort of artificial fibres that were designed to dry quickly. His hair, which had not been designed in such a way, was still damp. Without sitting up, he reached into his sandal for his watch.

He could hear the surf more clearly now, the breaking waves, the screams of children in the water. The tide was coming in. Seagulls swooped out of the sky around him. Earlier in the afternoon, one had taken a french fry out of his son's hand. Matty only shrugged and reached into the basket for another. He had a smear of red ketchup on his cheek. His hair was stiff with salt and sand. He wore bright orange water wings.

David squinted against the sun's glare off the face of his Timex.

They should prepare to leave, he thought.

A little further down the beach, his wife sat in a portable camp chair they had purchased at Canadian Tire. If he twisted his neck, he could just see her from the corner of his eye. Blue chair, white bandana. He thought he could make out the silhouette of Anne's foot. Her legs were crossed.

He couldn't help but think that the distance between them now was more than physical. The angle of Anne's shoulder was forbidding. Her neck rigid and stiff, in spite of the weather. The ocean. The family needed a vacation. But perhaps the road trip was a touch ambitious. The stress of plotting a route and then seeing it through to practical fruition was proving a bit much.

Cape May was a compromise on his part for Atlantic City. Yesterday, they had driven seven hours to arrive there. Or rather, he had driven seven hours. Anne and the kids were passengers. They stopped only twice. Once at a tourist information centre in the north of Pennsylvania on the Susquehanna, where they ate sandwiches prepared at home the night before, and posed in front of an old-fashioned steam engine for photographs. It was a small engine used for coal mining. David had always harboured an unspoken admiration for industrial technology in general, but trains in specific. Perhaps it was because he knew next to nothing about machines, or simply that he found their utility beautiful.

They stopped a second time just over the New Jersey border after Philadelphia. It was a massive rest stop complex on a hill with a gas bar and fast food restaurants overlooking the freeway. The heat off the asphalt parking lot almost seared his daughter's feet. Nat had removed her sandals in the van.

After they had used the toilets, Anne prepared a snack with apples and cheese from the electric cooler. Once, on a camping trip in Bon Echo, David had mistakenly left it plugged in overnight. Even though it only took ten minutes for their neighbour at the next campsite to boost their car, the line of Anne's jaw as she thanked them left no doubt in David's mind just how angry she was.

Anne doled out the food. They were all tired and cranky. Nat wanted McDonald's. Matty had just woken up from his nap and cried for no apparent reason. David's wife was losing patience, and inwardly he was disgusted with his family's lack of stoicism. He had high expectations of his children. The whine and thrum of the turnpike were like bees in his mind.

An hour later, however, they were on the beach, and everything seemed fine. The sun was low in the sky behind them, but still far from disappearing. The ocean was a steel grey. Anne took off her shoes and walked in the sand. She took pictures of the kids, the casinos, and an overturned fishing boat that had *Atlantic City* written upside down along its hull.

David noted that Anne was happy too. She hadn't yet seen the hotel.

It was a Best Western in the wrong part of town. The elevator was not working. The carpets had a funny smell, like boxwood, or wet dog. It was also double what they had expected to pay. David had noted the off-season rate on the Internet. July was peak season. He experienced that familiar shift in atmosphere that characterized his relationship with Anne. He used to think of it as something that he could control with the right word or gesture, but lately he had begun to feel differently. They still slept together, but they no longer kissed goodnight. He was not sure when they had stopped this tender ritual. More terribly, he could not imagine why. Now, more often than not, he would simply reach over and remove the book which lay on her face, set it on the floor beside him, and turn out the light. Her eyes having closed earlier, mid-paragraph.

He suggested supper on the boardwalk. Nat posed with a Russian dressed as a mermaid. Anne took the photograph while David pretended not to look at the mermaid girl's young lithe body, the nearly exposed breasts. With her turquoise mask, she reminded him of Carnival in Venice.

Matty asked to be carried. He was exhausted and couldn't keep up, so David swung him onto his shoulders. This only made Nat jealous, and she pouted until Anne bought her a mechanical dog from one of the many tourist stands.

The meal was awful, even though Anne tried to smile through it. It was a Chinese buffet, chosen more for its price than its culinary promise. The air-conditioning was too cold, and the wall-length window was grimy with sea salt and pollution.

On their way back along the boardwalk, Nat pointed out the giant Ferris wheel on the Steel Pier. Dusk was passing into darkness and the lights against the deep purple of the ocean sky beckoned. Music, like that from a shrill barrel piano, drifted vaguely over the crash of the surf. The way David saw it, the Ferris wheel was their last chance at salvation.

There were surprisingly few patrons. In short order, they were ushered into a gondola by themselves, and winding a slow rotation upward. Nat squealed and held her new mechanical pup tight to her chest. Matty buried his head in Anne's breasts. For almost a minute they were stalled and swinging in the sea breeze 250 feet from the deck while people boarded. It was vertiginous. David's feet ached each time Nat looked over the edge. And then the wheel began to spin its lazy clock-like reel.

Each time their gondola crested, the infinite stretch of the ocean at night opened before them. And a moment later, the cabin plunged earthward. Up and down the strand lights blared like an erratic airport runway and the screams from the more extreme rides wafted over the carnival melody. The decadence of it all made David think of Pompeii before Vesuvius—an arrogant coastal resort for the wealthy, holding back the sea.

David left his family at the hotel room later and purchased a bottle of rum at a convenience store down the street. He bought Coke as a mix. The gesture worked. With the kids asleep, Anne relaxed and they drank rum from plastic bathroom cups.

"We can't drive seven hours straight tomorrow," she said. "No," David agreed. He could tell that she was trying not to sound judgemental.

The plan was to cross New Jersey, Maryland, and Delaware on the way to Chincoteague, Virginia. Nat loved horses, and they were stopping to see the wild ponies. David read somewhere in one of the travel brochures that they were the descendants of English horses brought over by seventeenth-century settlers. The image used in the brochure showed several bloated animals. The caption explained that salt water in the grazing pastures forced the ponies to retain water. Anne complained often about retaining water, especially when she felt fat—which was increasingly the case. David had caught her contorting in the mirror, trying to gauge the gravity of love handles, or the cellulite on the backs of her legs.

"How about Wildwood or Cape May?"

"I don't know. Tell me about them."

David read aloud from a travel book called *Road Trip USA*. Their goal was Disney World, a destination he was not looking forward to, but the entrance tickets and five nights' accommodation were free. All they had to do was sit through a timeshare presentation. He had not yet mentioned this fact to Anne. While the idea of a vacation had been hers, the planning of it was David's job.

He suggested following the coast down. He was dreaming of Charleston and Savannah. He taught high school history, including a section of American history. He loved the Civil War. He hoped to stop in Gettysburg and Harper's Ferry on the way back. Another fact of which Anne was not yet aware.

In the end, she voted for Cape May. A Victorian village with a beach. She wanted to take in the sun. She wanted to read.

David rolled over and propped himself up on his elbows. On his belly, a small square impression had been left from the tag he had pinned there. An elderly woman under a parasol squawked at him earlier as he entered the beach beyond the earth-red snow fencing. You had to pay to use the beaches in New Jersey, she told him. And after he had, she gave him four blue tags to be worn at all times.

Anne was watching the kids tackle the waves, looking up periodically from her summer reading. She was wearing a one-piece swimsuit and a colourful sari to cover her legs, which she found embarrassing because of their cellulite spackling. Her hair was drawn back in a bun and held in place by her bandana.

"Anne," David called. Her head moved almost imperceptibly to the left. "It's almost four o'clock," he said.

They had to catch the Cape May ferry to Lewes. David had made reservations for four thirty the night before. Originally he had wanted to arrive in Chincoteague at that time. They were booked to stay at another Best Western just outside the National Wildlife Refuge. This one had a pool.

Anne sighed visibly and closed her book. All afternoon, David had played in the water with Nat and Matty. His wife gave him some respite a half hour ago, and pulled her chair closer to the water so that he could nap before taking the wheel again.

After deciding on Cape May, David and Anne had sex in the bathroom. It was quick and conciliatory. Anne sat on the counter beside the sink and wrapped her legs about his waist. She leaned back against the mirror, and accidently turned on the cold water tap with her elbow. David admired his wife's large breasts in the harsh light of the incandescent bulb and imagined himself as a daring and creative lover for about three minutes.

He reached over and turned on the fan just before he and Anne came together.

Sex, which had always been good between them, had also, of late, dwindled slowly into non-existence. Kids and work. Schedules that didn't mesh. Exhaustion. David chalked it up to life with a young family. It certainly wasn't a lack of interest on his part, though he suspected Anne might feel that way.

In response to his last overture, she'd said, "How can you still find me attractive?"

Honestly, he didn't even understand the question.

Back in the hotel room afterward, he felt happy again and he watched his children sleeping side by side in the double bed beside his own. Their little puckered mouths like precious flowers.

Anne called to the kids, and immediately Matty came running. Nat had thrown mud at him and he had it in his eyes, hair. David watched his wife clean the child. Then he lifted himself off the towel and began to gather the beach ware strewn about, packing the wicker bag Anne had purchased at Winners just for this purpose.

He hoped the ride to Chincoteague would be successful. And by that, he meant pleasant. It was important to him that the family remember this vacation fondly. That morning they had intended to stop in Margate to view Lucy the Elephant on their way to Cape May, but they drove past it the first time. It was a metal pachyderm six stories tall, and they had actually missed it. This was because of the fighting.

Anne wanted him to turn around so that she could take a photograph of someone's garden.

David balked, and that had set them off. Although he eventually returned, travelling the six blocks back through side streets, it was too late. He couldn't even remember what they were bickering about when they passed the elephant. It didn't matter.

Nat shouted to them, "Papa, you missed it."

David's playing with the children all afternoon had been his way of apologizing to Anne for not having turned around. This way she could read and relax in the sun, which was what she wanted to do. When she offered to relieve him later so that he could take a nap, this was her way of saying apology accepted.

David wrapped Matty in a towel as he came tripping over the sand. He lifted the boy, like a pupa, to his shoulder. He loved the way his son burrowed into things. It was as though his body, small as it was, had been conceived to fit into David's. His head at David's neck. His legs at David's waist. Although already four years old, he still sucked his thumb. David tried not to think of the future orthodontic bills.

He stared longingly over his son's shoulder at the wreck of the *Atlantus* silting in the shallows off the coast. He'd read about it only the night before, after Anne had drifted off to sleep. Its rust-coloured hull was now easily visible over the surf. Diving on the ship was apparently tricky. Though not deep, timing was of paramount importance. Swimming back to shore against the tides was virtually impossible. Back home he lived next to one of the world's greatest freshwater diving grounds and yet he had never managed to find the time to try it. Seeing the *Atlantus* caused the old desire to resurface. For more than a year, he'd been poking away at a book on the subject of St. Lawrence wrecks. A colleague had dumped a pile of research in his lap one afternoon and even offered personal diving lessons.

So little time. Or maybe it was more than that.

A moment later, he was pulled from his reverie. Anne was next to him, picking up the wicker bag in her free hand. The collapsed camp chair in the other.

"Where's Nat?" David asked.

Anne pointed toward the shore not far from where her chair had been.

"Well, she was there a second ago."

David placed Matty on the ground. The boy clung to his leg and would not let go.

"David, where is she? I don't see her."

The more unnerved Anne became, the calmer David tried to be. It was not a conscious effort on his part, just something his brain adapted to in an evolutionary way. Once Nat had fallen down the stairs to the basement in their home. Anne was in hysterics. She grabbed her hair and froze at the top of the stairs, screaming into the well. David moved her aside, skipped quickly past, and gathered the girl up. She was crying, but not wailing. Shocked more than hurt.

David held her to him. She was maybe three years old. She felt like a loaf of warm bread.

Later, after Anne was composed, it was David who called the nurse's hotline and made all the inquiries. Anne had written out all the questions on a pad of paper they kept by the phone, but it was David who called. He was good in an emergency.

"She must have gone back in to rinse off the mud," David said in an even, steady voice. "They were having a mud fight, remember?"

"I told her to look for my chair," Anne said. Her voice was rising. "She kept coming out of the water farther and farther down the beach. So I told her to use my chair to orient herself." Now Anne was walking. Pacing and then stopping.

David said, "Well, you've moved the chair. Maybe she wandered off that way looking for it." He looked in the direction he was indicating.

The family next to them must have sensed or heard that something was wrong, because the mother stood up and approached Anne. "Did you lose your daughter?"

"I don't know," Anne said. The women held hands. David didn't know who took whose hands first, but the women were holding hands now.

Matty sucked his thumb, oblivious. With his free hand, he played with the hairs on David's leg.

"She had on that pink bikini, right?" The woman sounded

like she was from New York. Her son had tried to kill a seagull with a baseball bat earlier in the day. The family was eating lunch and trying to fend off the birds. David thought it was odd that neither she nor her husband attempted to take the bat away from the boy.

"There's a lifeguard," the woman said, pointing in the direction David had just been looking.

The lifeguard was in his early twenties. A thick white mess of sunblock sat on the bridge of his nose. He had red hair, and he had tucked a red floatation device under his arm. David wondered if the fair-skinned boy ever regretted becoming a lifeguard.

"Don't worry, ma'am," he said to Anne. "This happens all the time. She probably just wandered off and can't find her way back. The beach is a crowded space."

"I told you," David said, also to Anne.

"Sir, why don't you walk that way toward the breakwater. We'll go this way. What colour was her swimsuit?"

Matty became fussy as David walked off toward the pile of rocks that extended out into the ocean like a finger. He refused to keep up, holding on to David's hand like an anchor.

"Stop it, Matty. This is not the time."

David was surprised by the sharpness of his own voice. He ruffled Matty's hair.

"You can watch a movie when we get back to the van," he said to mollify his son. They had rented a vehicle with a built-in DVD player in order to make the time pass more quickly for the kids.

"We're going to take a boat this afternoon," David added. He wasn't sure why.

And then he felt it. Panic. It was rising in his throat from some unknown place of origin. Beneath his heart, maybe. It was a tugging, as much as it was a rising. It felt as though he had swallowed a fishhook and now someone was dragging his insides toward the surface. He tried to swallow it down. To resist.

Then he looked at the ocean, as though for the first time. He saw kids splashing and playing. He saw surfers farther out, waiting for a wave. Nat had sworn earlier that there had been dolphins, but there was nothing now. David was looking for a spark of pink. He tried to tell himself that he was not looking for the floating body of his daughter. But he knew that he was.

He thought of the word *riptide*. He had read it in the travel book.

So this is how my life is meant to be, he thought. This is what tragedy feels like.

And then he became calm. But not like before. This was the cold stone of inevitability.

He looked across the sand and the sunbathers for his wife. Matty was pulling on his hand again. Before he could find Anne, a lifeguard blew a whistle. This is it, he thought. And then he saw her running. Lifting her sari and running. From where he stood, she looked so small and far away. Anne hated to run. She was touching her face and running. The lifeguard continued blowing until everyone slowly began to leave the water.

A City by the River

David and Anne lived in a modest high-ranch on the north end of town, beyond the freeway that pushed through the little city like a shunt. The freeway had ruined the historic downtown, and left the ugly offspring of convenience in its wake—fast-food chains, box stores, and the sprawling blight of a shopping mall. But it had also given birth to the suburbs where they lived.

Anne felt safe in the suburbs. She did not find them aesthetically pleasing in their redundancy. She would have preferred a little variety, a few more trees. But she was willing to sacrifice beauty for peace of mind. She was practical. The elementary school was only two blocks away. The secondary school, where her husband taught, was at the far end of their street. He could walk to work in good weather.

She could not begin to calculate the savings in fuel, insurance, and monthly loan payments.

If she did not consider the death of her daughter, more than a year ago now, then she could say things were proceeding according to plan. In fact, if she could only lose five or ten more pounds before next Christmas, things would be perfect. Wouldn't they?

Except she could not dismiss what happened to Nat. Sometimes she would pause at the front door of her home before leaving for work, convinced that she was forgetting something. She would return to the kitchen and touch the burners on the stove. Next she would make sure the coffee maker had been unplugged, the toaster. She would run upstairs and triple-check the lights in each room. Back in the front foyer, she verified her purse for keys, her cellphone.

Only after the circuit was complete would she realize that it was her daughter she was missing. Then she would cry softly. She didn't allow herself to cry for more than a few minutes, and afterward she would wash her face in the half-bath off the front hallway. She kept a bottle of Visine in the medicine cabinet there for such occasions, and diligently squeezed two drops into each eye before leaving.

Anne commuted an hour to Ottawa, and because her hours were erratic, she could not carpool. She worked in the parliamentary office of Gabriel Caulie, who happened to be the cabinet minister of the Department of Fisheries and Oceans. Gabe, as she now called him in private—in public everyone called him Minister—had hired her four years ago as an assistant to the legislative assistant, a job that did not pay much.

She had been working as a freelance translator for various medical journals and newsletters before that, including *CANNT* (Canadian Association of Nephrology Nurses and Technicians), which paid equally poorly and more sporadically.

The original legislative assistant, Patty McDonough, resented Anne's presence and her ease in both official languages. She once told Anne—which was actually short for Anne-Marie— that it was easier for francophones in Canadian politics, as they didn't have to force themselves to learn French. Anne guessed that either Patty assumed English was easier to learn, or that all Québécois were born with a genetic defect that allowed them to spontaneously break into foreign languages.

Each day, Anne's job was ostensibly to read clippings from Canada's French-language newspapers, which were provided to her from a communications office in the public service. She was to let Patty know of any issues the Minister might face during question period, so that she and the Minister could prepare possible responses. If the question was suspected to be asked by a member of the Bloc Québécois, or any other French-speaking Member of Parliament, Anne was asked to prepare the response, with the input of the Minister, in French.

Once Anne had learned the ropes on Parliament Hill, Minister Caulie—or Gabe—came to the realization that one bilingual candidate could perform the job of legislative assistant that was then being performed by two people. Anne found Patty crying in a bathroom stall the day Minister Caulie told her she was being moved to his constituency office in Corner Brook, Newfoundland.

Now Anne—or Anne-Marie, as only the Minister called her—worked as his legislative assistant and personal French tutor, which paid slightly more.

Anne found the Minister magnetic. He was handsome, though not unduly tall, with silver hair above his ears in a head of otherwise thick black hair. He was stocky, leaning toward heavy, but solid. He exuded power. Rumblings among the party faithful pegged him as future candidate for the prime minister's office. Of course, he'd have to learn French before that could ever happen.

Although the DFO was not a senior cabinet position like Health or Justice, Minister Caulie had successfully navigated the department through a whaling dispute with Iceland. In a rare show of force, he had the Canadian Coast Guard—also part of his portfolio—fire live ammunition over the bow of an Icelandic whaling frigate hunting illegally off the coast of Baffin Island in waters Canada claimed as its own.

Sovereignty over the North had recently become a hot topic for debate in the newspapers and during question period. Anne suddenly found herself, after years of quiet and methodical translation, at the heart thrum of the nation's political landscape.

One afternoon, Minister Caulie asked Anne how to say two-faced in French. He was angry about a comment from a French-speaking MP raised in the House of Commons the previous day.

"You would say a *visage à deux faces*," Anne replied. "But that is not at all a nice thing to say in French."

"Anne-Marie," Minister Caulie said, leaning over her shoulder.

"Yes, Minister." Anne liked the way he used her full name.

"Please, call me Gabe when we're in here."

"Oh," Anne said.

"These are tough times. And tough times call for tough language."

All this happened after Patty had returned to Corner Brook. Rumour in the office suggested that Patty and the Minister had been sleeping together. The same people who whispered about this affair also suggested that Patty needed to return to New-foundland before she started to show.

The Minister had a beautiful wife and four lovely children back home, and Anne refused to consider the Minister in this light. Even as he leaned in over her shoulder, ever so close.

David was the one to walk Matty to school each day. He had graduated from junior kindergarten the previous summer, and now he attended École Ste Marie de Grace full time. It was a small French school in a predominantly English-speaking community. The students wore blue uniforms and pressed white shirts. Matty was still at an age where he did not require a tie. But that would change in grade three.

David glanced down at his son's bleached head. The sun performed this magical transformation each year. It had been the same with Nat. Late at night in the basement, while Anne slept, David flipped surreptitiously through a photo album he had put together documenting their summer vacation from a year ago. The summer Nat drowned.

There were not many pictures in this album, as their vacation had only just begun, but already, in early July, his daughter's hair had turned a downy blonde. Not just the hair on her head, either. The wispy hairs on her forearms, legs, and shoulders changed as well. Even the pale dusting on her upper lip. David could not see this in the photos.

It was something he had committed to memory.

David had a good memory. Some people joked that it was practically photographic. Anne used to call him her walking encyclopedia. He had been proud of his memory. Now, ironically, he couldn't escape it. It had also been a long time since Anne called him that.

He and Matty had a ritual that they followed every morning at the front door of his school. David would say, "Well, here we are," and then he would ruffle Matty's hair. For his part, Matty would look up at his father and cry, "Huggy!" To which David would respond by bending down to his son's height and wrapping the boy in his arms.

This was meant to be a sign of their love. And Matty believed in their love then. Only each time David let him go, each time the boy turned, still looking backward over his shoulder until he needed his eyes to find his way further, David wondered if he believed in love any longer.

It broke David's heart to see his son this way, his eyes lingering on his father, squeezing everything possible from that moment. It broke his heart, because he knew that one day Matty would discover what David already knew. Everything eventually came to an end. Even love. And if it didn't end, it twisted and became sharp and ugly, and then you simply wanted it to end.

It was Matty's ignorance that crushed David. He could not yet see that his father had no love left. That he had grown miserly and mean as a way to protect himself from loss. Because hurt and pain were the measurement of love's depth. And David had experienced more of both than he cared to dwell upon.

At St. Lawrence Collegiate Institute, David taught history to students who couldn't remember yesterday, and he envied them as much as he hated them.

Once, and not so long ago, he had loved teaching as much as he loved his children. But now he didn't have children. He only had a child. Part of David realized it was just a question of semantics. Part of him understood it had nothing to do with semantics at all. At the same time that he could sense Anne tightening her grip on Matty, David could feel himself drifting. Turning his back.

The senior students in his Twentieth Century World History class still remembered the old Mr. Henry. The Mr. Henry who taught them Canadian history in grade ten. The teacher who had them strap on fifty-pound knapsacks and charge over makeshift trenches on the back field as classmates pummelled them with snowballs.

The Mr. Henry who had not lost a daughter to the sea.

These students slogged through his American history class the year before, and were sorry and understanding. They made allowances. He had, after all, just lost his daughter. But now they sat in desks that were too small for them, blinking and intent. They looked as though they were waiting for something to happen.

It was the new students from elementary schools across town

that made jokes at David's expense. Their rumours scuttled like cockroaches through the hallways on the lips of grade nine boys who had not yet reached puberty and wore pants too big for their hips.

You could smell the vodka on his breath, they said. Even through the peppermint Life Savers he sucked after lunch.

Others chastised, "You can't smell vodka. He's a rummy."

In a year or two, all traces of the teacher he used to be would be gone, and David would then cease to disappoint. There would be no expectations.

Anne awakened in the middle of the night. She could not breathe. It was as though a large cat was seated on her chest. She listened intently to the sounds her house made. Under the cat, her heart raced. She was listening specifically for Matty. Had he stopped breathing? she wondered.

The next-door neighbour's dog barked at a squirrel. Perhaps it was a rabbit.

Anne counted to ten, but her panic did not pass. She pulled off the duvet and placed her feet into the slippers by her bed. She took her nightgown from a hook behind the door. It was long and silky and it billowed as she moved quickly down the carpeted hall.

David complained about the way Anne walked all the time. "You thump," he said. "You walk on your heels, and you thump."

As a result, Anne tried to walk on her toes, so as not to awaken her husband. She passed Nat's room and, for a moment, she felt compelled to check inside. What if it was all just a terrible nightmare?

She stopped.

A twitch had been developing in her right eye of late. A small pulse of blood in her lower lid. It spoke to her. Told her to do strange things. Sometimes she resisted, but this only made her feel more anxious, so more often than not, she obeyed.

Yesterday, as she was drinking water from the cooler at work, it told her not to put the cup down until she had swallowed ten times. Later in the same day, during a meeting with staff from the communications department, she cleared her throat, and then had to clear it twice more once the twitch kicked in. People had stared.

Anne reached out and touched the door handle to Nat's room as the twitch requested. Then she was free to continue on to her son's room.

Matty slept with a nightlight. It was a recreation of Noah's Ark. He'd had it since infancy, and it matched the mural she and David had painted on the wall above his bed. Originally, this had been Nat's nursery. Anne leaned into the darkened room, now eerie in the sickly yellow wash of the nightlight. She watched her son's blankets for movement. He was fine, she thought. Her shoulders relaxed. She'd been grinding her teeth and now her jaw ached. Matty was fine.

Last Wednesday, she'd been convinced that something was wrong at Matty's school. She'd read somewhere in an issue of *Reader's Digest* that people too often ignore their intuition. The victim of a terrible car accident testified in the article that she hadn't paid attention to the little voice inside her head saying *don't drive today.* So Anne closed the door to her office and called Jocelyn, the secretary at École Ste Marie de Grace.

Everything had been fine then, too. Anne laughed and tried to explain about the article in *Reader's Digest*, but Jocelyn didn't sound convinced.

Anne's eye twitched again. It was worse when she was nervous. This time she tried to ignore its command. She rubbed it with her fingertips. She wanted to cry. Eventually, she had no choice but to give in. She had to work the next morning.

Anne reached out and tapped her son's door handle lightly. The same way she had tapped Nat's. Halfway down the hall, on her way back to bed, she paused, and then returned to tap the handle once more.

It was the twitch that told her to.

David took a walk along the river in Centennial Park. He kept the concrete retaining wall beneath his feet, and followed it like a path. Across the water was another country.

In the early summer students from his high school skipped class to swim here. Because of the depth of the current, the waters were always cold. Mostly, they came to parade new bathing suits and lie in the sun.

It was one of the largest rivers in the world.

People came from all over to dive on the St. Lawrence wrecks. Before Nat's death, David had been compiling documentation about the most popular maritime disasters. He had intended to write a book, at the behest of a persistent colleague. Part history, part guide for divers. The local bookseller on King Street assured him that no such book had ever been written, and that every summer dozens of tourists came in looking for one.

During his research, David had interviewed an eighty-eight-year-old local man named Everett Snider. Snider was the last surviving crew member of the *J.B. King*, a drill barge that had exploded off the Hillcrest shoal of Cockburn Island back in 1930. All day the crew had been setting charges of TNT deep in the river bed, when a freak lightning strike touched off the detonator on board. Snider had been thrown across the river by the force of the blast. When he surfaced, he realized that he was barefoot. He'd been blown clean out of his shoes. And his pockets were filled with coal from the coke boilers.

Originally, David had it in mind to take up scuba lessons as part of his research. An art teacher on staff had offered to take him out. But he'd forgotten about all that now.

It was October, and the air was cool. The dank musty smell of wet leaves permeated everything. The park was empty, but he'd been drinking at a downtown tavern all afternoon since the end of classes and needed to clear his head. Besides, he enjoyed the company of water, in spite of everything. Maybe, in some perverse way, it made him feel closer to Nat.

David had been a swimmer since the age of four. He'd learned on a river north of here. His mother used to take him during the week while his father was at work in Ottawa. His father, Larry Henry, worked for a computer firm. He was not a high-tech worker though. Even now, David didn't quite know exactly what he did. Accounting or contract negotiation, or some other such thing.

He couldn't ask him if he wanted. David hadn't seen his father since he was seventeen.

A tanker plied the river toward Kingston, destined for the Great Lake ports. Detroit or Chicago. Maybe Duluth. Its dark hull sleek as a rifle barrel.

Everything about David's father was a fairy tale. Like Peter Pan, he was the boy who refused to grow up. And as a young child, David thought that was marvellous. If his father took him to the sandpits to drive the car, he made him believe that they were driving into the moonshine country of the lower Appalachians, where you had to look out for bootleggers and rum-runners. David was never just a passenger in the car. He was riding shotgun, on the lookout for spies. Or Nazi informants. Or hostile Indians.

His father was worse than a writer. He was a dreamer. A man of could-have-beens and should-have-beens. And, of course, he was also a drinker. His constant gentleness, the polite mask he wore to face the world, hid a twisted violence. A demon who was tired of saying yes to his boss. Yes to his wife. Yes to his mother.

David only fully understood the existence of this doppelgänger one evening in his last year of high school. His mother and his father had been arguing. Which meant that Larry had been drinking. David was in his room, feigning doing homework. It had not been a particularly bad argument. In fact, after a few minutes, David thought that it was safe to escape.

Downstairs his mother was not speaking. Only the red ember of her cigarette gave her silhouette any definition. She still smoked back then. But as David approached the kitchen, he heard a strangled, muffled sound. A cartoon gargling. He did not have the time to think more than that. He was in the kitchen only a moment later, and there, in the fluorescent screaming of the track lights, was his father. The man was kneeling with his head down, almost as though he were a runner awaiting the gun to take off. But under the weight of his right shoulder, in the grip of his fist, was the family cat. Pinned to the floor by its neck.

The gargling sound had stopped. But for an occasional spitting, the cat made no sound. Silently its back legs flicked and slipped on the vinyl flooring.

David could not remember what he yelled, but he did yell. In response, his father released the wretched creature. It slouched away slowly and crookedly, like a somnambulist. Larry, all the gentleness returned to him, stood like a child, shivering in the middle of the kitchen. The bright lights bleeding his skin pale.

When David returned from school the next day, his mother was crying at the kitchen table, only feet away from where his father had nearly strangled the cat. He was gone, she said. She didn't expect him back.

Disappearances were nothing new to David. It was his mother who watched him walk across the stage, alone, a few months later at commencement. And before he was finished university, she would leave him too. Metastatic carcinoma.

His last memory was of her swimming in a pool of morphine, jaundiced and gurgling on a tube. Unaware he was even in the room.

He had been angry with his father for a long time after he left. But he could have really used him in that moment.

When he looked up from his reverie, he was surprised to find someone in his path. He was almost upon her, yet she did not appear to notice him approaching.

David thought he recognized her from the high school. She had never been his student. He was sure of that. But it was a big school and there were many students who would have completed their time at SLCI without ever having taken a class from David.

She was slender, with bad posture. She slouched, hips pressed forward, torso back, as though she were attempting to look at something in the air above her. Only her shoulders folded back in upon her so that in silhouette she looked like the end of a violin.

Her hands were dug deep into the pockets of her jacket, and she gazed out across the river at the shifting colours of New York State.

The tanker David had spotted earlier was gone.

If he proceeded any further, he would run into her, so he stopped. That was when she noticed him.

She had a long pretty face, dark straight hair to her shoulders. Her coat looked like a retro ski jacket from the seventies. Light-blue with two slender white ribbons down each arm. It wasn't new.

"Hey." Her smile made her look vulnerable, as though the gesture might just as easily produce tears. But David could also tell that she recognized him. Seeing a teacher out of context often confused students. It was as though a life beyond the classroom had never occurred to them before. They were unsure what set of protocol to follow.

Sarah Evans. The name materialized out of nothing. She was in Rebecca Beames's grade twelve history class. A general level class, which meant, more than anything else, that she wasn't an overachiever.

Any time David walked past, the place was a zoo. But Sarah didn't strike him as the sort to act out. She was pretty enough, but clearly reclusive.

He was aware that she missed a lot of school because he'd heard Rebecca grumbling over it while entering attendance into the computer.

"Hey," David replied. He was suddenly self-conscious about being drunk, but also a little cavalier.

"Didn't see you at school today." Which was true, but not abnormal.

Sarah blushed and searched David's face for sarcasm. "I was at work."

"Oh." David was at a crossroads. He could stay, or he could leave. Either choice would be awkward for different reasons. He should have stopped at Hey.

"Over at the motel." She shrugged in the direction of Highway 2. "I clean rooms, but only when I'm needed. I also work at the Dunkin' Donuts on 29. But I don't get many hours."

She had pale, almost translucent skin beneath her cheeks, where tiny blue tracks criss-crossed like the cracks in a windshield.

"Saving for college?"

"I want to be a flight attendant. Maybe live out west."

David nodded.

"I'm sorry about your daughter, Mr. Henry."

It had been a long time since David had heard anyone offer

him their condolences. Nat had been gone more than a year and her death was still the event that defined him. He suddenly knew it would always be like this. He, and everyone around him, would delineate his history as before and after Nat.

He thought he might cry.

A car drove by without a muffler. It drew looks from both of them.

"Well, I should be getting home."

He turned toward the street and walked across the grass. "Don't work too hard," he yelled over his shoulder.

David could tell from the quality of light that it was growing late, and Matty would be worried if he did not make it home for supper.

Anne straightened the fringe on the imitation Turkish carpet in the living room. She had purchased it at Ikea against David's wishes, and now it mocked her. Originally, the rug's intricate geometry—its subtle perfection—had soothed her. Now, each time Matty tore through the room, the fringe was displaced. It didn't matter how many times she stooped to flatten and stretch it out. Someone or something always came along and messed it up.

She stood and placed her hands on her hips. Out the window to her left, she could see David and Matty on the front lawn. She could never understand how he did it. She almost never felt compelled to play.

David tossed the baseball toward Matty, who flinched, held the glove out in self-defence, and turned his head. The ball landed at her son's feet and skipped between his legs.

The sprinkler was running in the yard across the street. It was an Indian summer.

Anne had often felt underappreciated by her children. They

gravitated toward David with a sureness that pained her. He was all about fun. The claw. Tiger attack.

Spin me! Spin me!

But it was Anne who scheduled the dentist appointments, saw to regular physicals and immunizations. Anne who signed the permission forms. She made sure that the lunches were healthy and that the kids had canned preserves during school food drives. She had been waiting for her children to grow up and realize this, to discover the wonderful mother that she was to them.

Anne watched as the ball rolled into the street and Matty chased after it. It was as though someone had punched her. But the boy simply bent at the waist, picked it up, and came trundling back to the lawn. The late-day sun lit up his hair like a candlewick.

Anne moved into the kitchen to fix supper.

Part of her was glad to have David. It relieved her. But another part of Anne resented him. This part of Anne suspected her husband of a casual campaign to undermine her. Sometimes while her children clamoured for his attention, Anne just wanted to lock herself in the bathroom and cry.

She had made efforts with Nat. Together they had planted a Fairy Garden in the backyard. They had spent the better part of an afternoon gathering plants from Anne's various perennial beds and then transplanting them in a special bed beside the back shed. They constructed a bower and decorated it with plastic fairies purchased at the dollar store. Anne found the idea in a children's book, and while Nat had been reticent at first, by the end she was excited, running off to her bedroom or the toy box for items to embellish their creation.

Anne took a tomato from the refrigerator and placed it on a wooden cutting board.

She had felt as though that garden was going to change

things. She couldn't imagine all that had been stolen from her since. The injustice of it.

For a long time, Nat believed she was a horse. She paraded through the house at a gallop. Stomping and champing. Flicking her head from side to side. And then bolting, as she imagined a mustang might behave.

She performed this pantomime most frequently in the gardens. Constructing a path through the various beds of Anne's creation, past the Fairy Garden they built together. Her hair was finally long and hanging past her shoulders. Anne could barely pull a comb through it. Most days it was knotted and wild, and it suited Nat. During her games, Nat would pause, lifting her chin to the wind, the way a horse might sniff out danger and then snort at her imaginary discovery. Shaking her head, Nat would burst away in a foal-like leap, so real that at moments even Anne believed in the act.

"Am I fast?" she used to ask. "Do I look like a horse?" And then she'd have Anne time her as she ran, horse-like, through the course she had designed. It was a kind of skipping more than a run. Anne had seen lemurs perform the same way on the Discovery Channel.

"Thirty seconds," Anne declared.

"Was that good?"

"Very good."

Anne was sure to knock a few seconds off at different intervals, sometimes rewinding the imaginary clock to keep her daughter determined. If she were trying to read, or nap in her chair, the constant requests might become onerous. But mostly, Anne enjoyed the game. Somewhere deep inside she knew these were the moments that would make up her life in the end. And that she should savour them. These were the reasons, beyond biology, that one had children.

When Nat discovered the noise flip-flops made, her creation

was complete. In late summer afternoons, Anne would sit on the deck with a glass of wine counting the time to the miraculous snap of hoof-like feet.

The tomato blurred as Anne's eyes filled with water. She felt the sharp edge of the knife sink into the taut flesh of the fruit. Then she heard the screen door slam and her heart skipped. The blade bit a second time with the same assurance, carving a fine line into the knuckle of her index finger.

The pain was absolute.

"*Maman!*"

"Just a minute." Anne did not recognize her own voice. It produced a high-pitched warble, a prelude to hysteria. She snatched at the tea towel hanging beneath the sink.

"*Maman! Maman!* I catched it. I catched the ball!"

As she rounded the corner on the far end of the living room, she saw her son standing victorious with his arm raised. In the glove was the evidence of his catch.

She almost smiled before she noticed the carpet beneath his feet, the dishevelled fringe.

The towel in her hand was red all the way through. Her eye, which had been quiet all day, began to twitch. She bit her lip and cried.

The principal called him into the department office. Rebecca Beames answered the phone. David could tell by the self-righteous way she passed him the receiver that his boss was furious, and not up to concealing this fact.

That his old friend Paul Whitcomb was angry did not worry David. He only wished that it had not been Rebecca who answered the call. She was a relatively new teacher, and younger than him by about five years. She was not popular with students or other teachers. In spite of her youth, she rubbed kids the wrong way. She was too severe, and she held grudges. Rebecca also favoured female students to the detriment of boys in her class. Each semester she took on a new pet, spent lunch hours with her, swapped gossip, and went on outings to buy classroom materials for projects like bulletin boards and sock puppets. This student invariably discovered the woman's shallow narcissistic vacuity, which resulted in tears on both sides and an adolescent heartbreak.

She'd been observing David's nervous breakdown with a certain *schadenfreude*, and now she smelt blood. Looking at her, he thought she might actually pee herself with happiness.

"Tell me you did not threaten to kill Ryan Lefebvre." Principal Paul Whitcomb, a former colleague of David's in the history department, sat on the far side of his desk rolling two Chinese stress balls in the palm of his right hand. The gentle tinkle they produced reminded David of wind chimes.

He had not even entered the room yet.

"I did not threaten to kill Ryan Lefebvre."

Paul had thin brown hair that was receding like glaciers in Antarctica. He was one of the good guys. He'd made a terrible decision entering administration. Politics confused him, and his idea of discipline was a stern talking-to. David was sorry to have put him in this position.

"Well, he says you did. Got two or three others lining up to corroborate." The stress balls sounded more like a rusty swing set now. Paul's tie was already pulled away from his neck. His shirt gaped at the collar.

"Says you called him stupid, as well."

David was actually surprised at how astute the Lefebvre kid had been in interpreting his remarks. He suspected the boy came from a long line of mouth-breathers. Go back two generations and the boy's ancestors might not have yet walked upright.

David shrugged. "I told him if he'd been born in ancient Sparta his parents would have abandoned him on the slopes of Mount Taygetus. They'd have been within their legal rights."

"Sit down," Paul demanded. He tossed the balls into a drawer and wiped his face with his hands.

"Dave. You've got to pull it together, man."

David nodded in agreement. He could see Paul was at a loss. David was also half in the bag, and not up to arguing. He kept a bottle of rum in a locked filing cabinet.

"I know you've been hurt. God, I remember the funeral like it was yesterday." Paul looked at his hands, which were open, palms up on his desk.

This made David look too.

"But it wasn't, Dave. It wasn't yesterday. It's been what? Eighteen months? Kids are starting to talk, man. Your colleagues, too. I tell you this as your friend. I'm getting calls, Dave. From parents."

Paul sat back in the plush of his ergonomically designed rolling chair. It hissed with the expulsion of air. They used to play basketball together before Nat died. Thursday night men's league in the school gym.

"Lefebvre says he can smell the vodka off you each time he has your class after lunch."

David nodded again. Paul was awful from the field, but he worked the boards well.

He sprang forward suddenly, gripping the edge of his desk. "Well? Is it true?"

"Don't be ridiculous, Paul." David looked his friend straight in the eye. "You can't smell vodka. It doesn't have a scent."

They were in the limousine on their way to Parliament Hill. It was only Anne and Gabe and Danny Cummings in the back. Sébastien Latouque was their new driver. He often hung around Anne's office when the Minister didn't need him. He'd been chauffeur to Pierre Trudeau and he liked to tell racy stories. Anne figured this was his way of hitting on her. He wasn't very smart.

Nobody called him by his real name. They shortened it to Bass, like the fish. He was the same age as the Minister. Same birth date. He pointed that out to Anne during one of his visits. It only proved, to Anne, what the ravages of cigarette smoke could do to a body. His skin had a sallow tinge. His face was flecked with liver spots, and his hair was thin and greasy. He wasn't nearly as youthful or healthy in appearance as the Minister. There was a window between the front and back seats and it was up, so Bass couldn't hear the three of them talking in the rear.

"Nobody's talking about fish now, Gabe." Like Anne, Danny was one of the few people who could address the Minister by his first name and get away with it. He was also a Newfoundlander from Corner Brook. He'd studied political science at Memorial University, and was Gabe's executive assistant.

Danny Cummings and Anne were the only two people within the Minister's inner circle who were not actually related to him in some way. Gabe's older brother Sydney ran the office on the Hill. His uncle Tate was his political advisor.

Anne got the impression that Danny Cummings did not like her. His last outburst had interrupted her conversation with Gabe. She was trying to get the Minister to say the French "r" properly. "It's like you're preparing to spit," she said.

The moment Anne heard Danny Cummings speak, her left eye twitched. Neither he nor Gabe noticed as she cleared her throat and then picked non-existent lint off her blouse. Twice.

"Christ, Danny," Gabe exploded. "Sorry, Anne-Marie." He turned and laid his hand on her thigh and looked at her seriously.

Her eye twitched several times in quick succession. The Minister wore a cologne that reminded her of freshly cut grass and summer afternoons.

"Are you okay?"

Anne cleared her throat and smoothed the crease in her pant leg. "I'm fine."

"We've got to find a way to weigh in on this referendum question," said Danny. His eyes fluttered in Anne's direction for a moment. She had just cleared her throat twice more.

Danny Cummings was overweight and did not cut his nails. He may have been a wunderkind in the political world, but Anne could not picture him as a politician. She looked out her window as the car turned onto Wellington and tried to ignore what her twitch was whispering to her.

Matty is fine. Matty is fine. Matty is fine.

She fingered the cellphone in her coat pocket.

"Listen, Danny. If and when fishing rights in the St. Lawrence come up, we'll take a stand. But I don't think it's going to be a make-or-break issue in the debate over an independent Quebec. Let it go. We pick our fights."

Danny Cummings leaned forward. "I don't think you understand how close this thing's going to be." Then his voice went low. "If you make some sort of gesture—an olive branch kinda deal—and the No side wins by a slim margin, it's gonna look like it was you that tipped the scales. The Prime Minister isn't going to be prime minister forever, and no one's interested in the heir apparent."

Danny's breath smelled like stale coffee and bacon grease.

"You're the dark horse here, Gabe."

Anne glanced over at the Minister. He was staring at the floor. "Tell Bass to swing over to Elgin. I need a minute to think this through."

"What if the Yes side wins?"

"Impossible." Danny Cummings waved his hand in a way Anne found effeminate. "And even if the impossible were to happen, you come out looking like the only guy who tried."

"What's that, Anne?" Gabe and Danny Cummings were looking directly at her.

Had she said something? She cleared her throat. She must have cleared her throat.

"You should go to Montreal," she said.

Danny Cummings rolled his eyes and sat back shaking his head.

"Hold a pro-Canadian rally," she continued, making things up as she went. Danny Cummings had a smug face she wanted to slap, and, she thought maliciously, he was balding prematurely.

"Forget it. Even if you got a crowd out, the PQ would spin it on Radio Canada until it looked like a handful of out-of-touch old-boy Empire Loyalists from Westmount having tea while the *Titanic* was sinking around them."

"Just a minute, Danny." Gabe held his hand up for silence. "Go on, Anne-Marie. I'm listening."

Anne held her finger up to her eye. "Invite people from across Canada. Who wouldn't want to see Montreal for a weekend?"

"Yes." Gabe was nodding. Even Danny Cummings was quiet. Big Daddy's Crabshack skated past outside behind the Minister's head.

"And we'll fix it with the air carriers. It's beautiful. Call the whip's office, Danny. Tell her we won't be there for question period."

Gabe looked at Anne. "How soon can you be ready to go to Montreal?"

"Me?"

"I'll have to give a speech. Got to be in French."

Matty is fine. Matty is fine. Matty is fine.

"Hey, is there something in your eye?"

When David and Matty were asleep in their beds, Anne stood in the pale glow of her Gibson refrigerator and shovelled food into her mouth. Mostly she ate leftovers, swallowing them snake-like and whole. She figured David, who couldn't stand leftover food, would never notice their disappearance. She hated herself during these moments.

But in a perverse way, she revelled in her weakness. She couldn't stop herself from spearing the next cube of meat or twirling more spaghetti around the end of her fork. She imagined she could feel herself gaining weight. Fat settling on her hips and in the soft flesh at the base of her ass.

It was a punishment she felt she deserved.

Lately she had taken to drinking meal-replacement shakes in an effort to lose weight. Over the years she had tried everything. But the shakes were her favourite. There was an emptiness about them that pleased her. She liked the gritty undissolved chunks of powder that stuck in her teeth like flavoured sand. She always felt hollow after drinking one. Scooped out.

It reminded her of how she felt back in high school after purging or a bout of Ex-Lax-induced diarrhea.

She'd been a member of the varsity volleyball team. No one would guess that about her now, she thought. She was slowly being swallowed by fat.

Her clothing squeezed her, bit into her ballooning breasts, and left red imprints in the skin at her waist. She was tattooed by the fabric.

And she was convinced that David found her repulsive. He had not touched her since Nat's death. They barely spoke anymore. And when they did, Anne felt as though they did so through a clear plastic coating that muffled sound and sensation.

When the food was gone, Anne would return to bed and listen to David snore. She caught the whiff of barbecue sauce on her own breath, and was pleased with self-loathing. She dared to touch herself then, imagining the gritty goodness of meal-replacement shakes.

After a few minutes, she dissolved into their perfect emptiness.

The van idled outside the CPR station house on Pearl Street. David was silent in the driver's seat. Anne ran through a checklist written on a pad of paper in her lap.

"There are casseroles and pizza in the freezer," she said finally.

David nodded. Two young men in ripped jeans walked past the hood of their vehicle. One of them wore a toque, even though the sun was out and the air was warm. Beyond the youths, David could see the overpass and the rooflines of vehicles shuttling across in both directions. Beneath it were the rail barns, piles of ties like toxic fingers. It was a small station, and growing smaller. People didn't travel by train much anymore. They didn't recognize the romance in it. Not that he and Anne were exactly Cooper and Hepburn in *Love in the Afternoon.*

There were a lot of ways to leave this place, David thought.

Anne sighed and opened the passenger door. Noise poured in. A woman pushed a clattering baggage cart toward the station entrance. Tires screeched and a muffler roared as someone pulled away from the lot behind them.

Matty was buckled into his booster seat behind Anne. He looked up, a plastic figurine in each hand. Ninja turtles.

"Is *Maman* going now?"

David remembered driving home from his grandmother's house a child, lying in the back window, racing the moon. New child safety laws in Ontario meant that his son would be strapped into a harness until he was old enough to drive.

The side door slid open. Anne peeked in.

"I'll be back on Monday," she said. "That's three days."

David watched as she took Matty's face in both hands, kissed him.

The boy pouted.

"I'll bring you home a new Transformer," she promised, glancing down at his hands.

Matty smiled. "*Maamaan*! These are ninjas."

"Oh."

David stepped out of the van and walked around to the back hatch. Across the street, people were lining up at the Loaves and Fishes building. They would be preparing supper at the food bank.

He extracted his wife's bag, which was extraordinarily heavy. It was part of a set her father had given them years ago as a wedding present. They had taken the bags with them to England. He shook his head to think about it.

They'd left at nine o'clock from Ottawa on the evening of their wedding. They were excited but exhausted. On the flight a man in the aisle seat across from David drank too much. He paraded up and down the plane praying in Arabic, throwing his arms in the air.

Later, after the steward managed to seat the man, he began to tap David on the arm. His persistence bothered Anne, who was trying to sleep against David's opposite shoulder. Uncharacteristically, David exploded, which brought the steward and a host of stewardesses running. When the dust settled, David and Anne were presented with a two-litre magnum of champagne, courtesy of Air Canada.

They drank the bottle two nights later at a bed and breakfast in Oxford, over herring pâté and bread. They were flushed with their success in piloting the little manual-shift Vauxhall. It was the first time they made love as husband and wife.

David lifted the bag to the platform outside the station door and turned to face Anne.

"You'll take good care of him?"

David sighed. In the past, he might have made a poor joke,

but he no longer had the right. When they kissed, it was just another lie they told themselves to help them get along.

David dreamed of water. He dreamed he was deep in the St. Lawrence River with an oxygen tank on his back. He was following another diver several metres below him into the green-grey fluid gloom. They were approaching eighty feet when they noticed scattered debris. Metal winch cables, slabs of corroded iron.

Farther down, they swam past the broken heart of a boiler. It was the wreck of the J.B. King. There had been two boilers aboard the drill barge, and 200 tons of coal. Chunks of the element lay strewn like road apples over the river bed.

The sunlight penetrating through at this depth was weak. By the time David slipped past the 120-foot mark the water was black. The current ripped across the rock ledge and out into the Seaway. He felt terror rising in his chest, like a familiar ghost.

A moment later, the other diver materialized over his shoulder. David felt a tug on his oxygen line, hands on his mask. He struggled to shake the diver off without success. The panicked swimmer had the strength of desperation and fear.

They were rising now, toward a bubble of light on the surface. David imagined nitrogen bubbles expanding in his blood-stream. In the distance he could hear the low grumbling purr of a tanker. In one last desperate attempt to save himself, David pulled loose his assailant's line. The water bubbled with the release in pressure. The diver's tank bled into the atmosphere around them.

In a moment of confused calm, the other diver stared through the gloaming with eyes wide. David recognized immediately that it was his Nat, frozen with panic. He fumbled again for her hose. The neurons sang in the space behind his ears. His fingers would not respond.

Inexplicably, she began to float away from him into the throbbing heart of the river. He screamed, but no sound escaped.

Awake and shivering in his bed, David recalled the afternoon two boys dragged his daughter's body up the interminable length of beach to the first-aid station in Cape May. She swung between them like a wet rope hammock. Her eyes were partially open and this fooled David for an instant and flooded his senses with false hope. Anne had begun a high-pitched keening, and two men were called upon to keep her back as the lifeguards commenced CPR.

David worried about the placement of her legs. They were turned in a way that would have hurt her. Scratch marks bloomed fresh and vivid on her belly. There was sand in her nose.

Outside the centre of the circle, the crowd was uncannily silent. Matty stood very still, his nose running and his little feet working in the muck.

On the far side of where Nat lay stood the boy with the bat. It dangled limp from one hand and rested at an angle in the beach. David felt the urge to seize it then, to feel the heft of it in his hands like a reassurance of the solidity of the world. He wanted to swing away with the weight of it, until every living thing around him lay pulverized and broken.

He wanted to die.

David had not touched Anne since the week after the funeral. She thought about this as her train rocked toward Ottawa. The flowers from the wake, gathered into bushes in the living room, were just beginning to wilt. Both she and her husband avoided that room since the reception. They did not need the precocious beaming of the blooms. She turned toward him beneath the sheets. Sex had been the last thing on her mind, but David read this as an overture. The sudden closeness. When he touched her, his hand grazing the side of her breast on its way to her hip, Anne felt a small awakening. It shocked her. She had felt nothing for days.

There was no pretence of foreplay. She rolled onto her back, lifting the sheets for David. Her legs, after years of habit, were already parted. David slid the crotch of her panties aside before positioning himself over her.

He grunted. They both did.

But the moment he was inside her, something in Anne died. David's penis, blunt and insistent, could have been a kitchen utensil. He felt it too. She could tell.

Both of them struggled on. Uncharacteristically, David could not ejaculate quickly. It was like a forced march. At first, Anne just lay there waiting for it to end. But as David dragged on, she moaned and coaxed him with her hands on his buttocks. Feeling encouraged by the change in his breathing, Anne played up the charade, until she began to cry.

When their eyes met, what Anne saw was hatred looking back at her. She thought David might roll off her then. But he did not. His breath came in short rough bursts, timed with each thrust.

When he finally came, David did not collapse or wait until he shrunk inside her, as he often did. Instead, he withdrew quickly and left the room.

Anne could feel the sperm leaking out onto her thigh. She squeezed her legs tight together so that she would not sully the bed. After David did not return, she made her way to the ensuite bath to clean up.

Outside the train window, small plots of farmland dragged into the distance. The wildflowers by the tracks' edge were a purple blur.

Amos had the index finger of his right hand buried knuckle-deep in his nose. David tried not to look. He viewed the locally developed history programme as a form of penance. He taught most of the senior history courses and supplemented those with academic classes at the intermediate level. His one burden was the essentials class. Most of them had individualized learning plans—which meant that they had numerous learning disabilities, often severe, coupled with behavioural disorders.

Fortunately, the class size was capped and rarely exceeded a dozen kids anyway.

"Careful, Amos," teased a classmate. "You might stab your brain."

Amos had had his head shaved recently after a bout of lice. His skin was waxy and riddled with blackheads. Most days he wore a large hockey jersey advertising the San Jose Sharks—not because he liked them, but because it was available at the Goodwill. David doubted that the jersey had ever been washed.

Jessica Pohlman turned just in time to catch the boy withdrawing the guilty digit. "Gross."

The rest of class laughed, except for Michele, who looked down and away, and then eventually out the window.

Michele was Amos's unfortunate desk mate. On the class list, next to her name, it read MID—an acronym for *mildly intellectually disabled*. Ordinarily, she would have been placed in a different class altogether—Room 110, as it was known colloquially to the staff. It was the equivalent of a special education room from a decade or two earlier, where the kids followed a curriculum of life skills. This meant baking and collecting the attendance during the home form period. They often went for walking trips downtown as well. Stopping into local businesses for demonstrations. But Michele's parents were among the more proactive. They wanted real credits and a high school diploma at the end of four years.

David knew, however, that she could not read, and would never pass the mandatory literacy test she'd be taking in the spring.

Nonetheless, she was one of the bright lights in his class. She was quiet, unobtrusive. She did her work, or tried. And she partnered with Amos during group work.

Leonard Castleman snickered into the screen of his computer long after the joke had passed. He was slouched deep in his chair—his head half-hidden, turtle-like, in his winter coat. It was a balmy fall afternoon, but he'd be wearing the coat well into May or June. It hid the fact that he owned only one T-shirt.

Leonard was a frequent disruption, but if David had a favourite, it was Leonard. Aside from history class, Leonard was enrolled in wood shop, automotive technology, and welding. He frequently brought his tech projects to class to show David, including a beautiful hand-carved cedar paddle with a wood-burnt design. He was good with his hands.

David approached the boy from behind. "Does this have anything to do with your assignment?"

Leonard promptly collapsed the window, revealing a blank slideshow presentation. The cursor blinked in the top left-hand corner of the screen.

A lone earbud dangled from the left side of the boy's head. He had a mop of auburn hair, poorly cut. His features were exaggerated. Thick lips, large eyes with long lashes. He was small but wiry, with heavy fingers and oversized hands.

"Sorry, Mr. Henry." Leonard had a nasal way of speaking, as though his nose were constantly plugged.

It was a good day.

David could read the boy like a weather forecast if he paid attention. He was a barometer for the entire class—which today had only eight students.

Room 219 had been cleaved off the end of a larger room several years earlier and was now sandwiched in between two computer labs. Along one wall, a bank of blinded windows opened into one of those rooms. There was a door as well, but it was locked and obstructed by an ancient laser printer. It was not an ideal setup, as sometimes kids in the other room would tap on the glass and disrupt the class. Or, as more often happened, David's students would play with the blinds and pull faces at those working diligently during their computer time.

The thirteen students officially on David's roll normally sat around a pool of tables in the middle of the room, but the benefit of being in the cramped space was having daily access to the ten computer terminals spaced out against three walls.

David turned and completed a lazy stroll around the tables. The remaining students were completing a word search about the "Roaring Twenties." It was busy work. And David knew it.

Ordinarily, he'd have been assigned an educational assistant to help with accommodations, but he didn't want anyone's judging eyes to witness his increasingly lackadaisical approach. And Melinda Branch, the school's head of Special Education, whose resources were already stretched, was only too willing to leave David to it.

A successful period used to mean something more to him. But seventy-two minutes without incident was his new litmus test.

Without warning, Jessica Pohlman leapt to her feet and ran to the door. "You're here!"

It was a melodrama David had almost grown used to. Jessica Number Two had arrived. Twenty minutes late.

"Hey, babe."

The two girls embraced like exhausted boxers. Ironically, they shared the previous class as well.

Jessica Burnam-Long was commonly referred to as a hall lizard. A student who attended school, but not class. Periodically, Corey Sharp, the vice principal and head football coach, would go on a week-long binge clearing the halls of their numerous lizards. But ultimately, they were left alone. In a school with just over a thousand students, it was impossible for one man to be both policeman and instructional leader.

Jessica Number Two was a thorn in David's side. When she did elect to attend, she rarely made it much past the classroom threshold. She did not bring books. She did not own a pen or a pencil. Although these last two facts did not differentiate her from the others.

On a good day, she would sit on the floor, just inside the door, and listen to her music. Ostensibly answering questions from the textbook. On a bad day, she enlisted the help of Jessica Pohlman to harass Amos, or worse—Leonard Castleman. Today, like most days, she wore a T-shirt advertising a band David had never heard of and a pair of dark stretch pants. She also favoured high-top basketball sneakers, though she had not likely ever held a basketball.

Jessica Number Two announced louder than necessary, "I just saw Leonard's sister in the breezeway."

David closed his eyes. He was definitely going to need a drink.

"Fuck you." Leonard was standing, fists clenched, his earbud swinging from the headphone jack of his computer. His chair slowly tipped and toppled backward until it clattered against the aged metal radiator system running beneath the outdoor windows.

Leonard's "sister" was a grade twelve student, and his name was Clarence. At least in the school register. In grade eleven, he requested that his teachers call him Clarisse, and he began to paint his nails.

This past September, he showed up on the first day of school wearing a tank top and skirt. Despite its quasi-urban location, St. Lawrence Collegiate Institute was a decidedly rural school in a markedly conservative area of Ontario. It did not have many students like Clarisse. And it wasn't easy on the ones it did have.

"Jess," David warned, "take a seat."

"Someone's on the rag."

Leonard was not likely to hit a girl, no matter how angry, but David did not want to take the risk. Surprisingly, family meant a lot to Leonard—as did family pride.

"Jess," David repeated.

"You're such a slut." This came out of nowhere from Tamara Burtch. She was a heavy-set girl with excessive makeup, repeating the year after failing history the spring before. The outburst was uncharacteristic, but like Leonard, Tamara was a tough customer.

"I don't have to put up with this shit. Come on, Jess. Let's go."

Jessica Pohlman looked at David and then back to her friend. She licked her lips. A moment later the doorway was empty and David could hear the girls laughing as they ran down the hallway.

Leonard brushed past next on his way out the door, but at that exact moment Sarah Evans happened to be passing and the two collided. Sarah stumbled and then toppled, breaking her fall with her left hand. Her head struck a locker across the corridor.

David skipped past the startled students. But already Leonard was bent over helping the girl to her feet. The boy was mortified. "Shit. Man. Sorry. Shit." His face was drained of all its colour. He'd hit a girl after all. An older girl. An older, attractive girl.

David watched as Sarah recovered and commenced laughing.

"Are you all right?" he offered.

Leonard snorted. "Shit." He too was laughing, relieved and perhaps a bit excited.

"Leonard, please. Stop swearing." David felt like an idiot. He didn't know what to do with his hands. "Look. Leonard. Why don't you go back inside and work on your slideshow?"

"I'm really sorry." The boy was smitten.

"It's okay. I'm okay."

Once he'd meandered back, pulling up his jeans as he went, David turned to Sarah.

She'd been sent out of Rebecca Beames's class and was on her way to Mr. Sharp's office.

"What did you do?"

She brushed the bangs from her eyes and back behind her ear. "It's what I didn't do."

From what David could gather, the altercation surrounded an incomplete assignment, coupled with an insufficient level of prostration.

"I hate that fucking class." Her eyes grew huge, and her hand flew involuntarily to her mouth.

David just ignored the outburst. "Why not drop it, then?"

Sarah shrugged and looked at the ceiling. "I need a senior social science to graduate and it's too late in the semester to switch."

David nodded. If he stayed in the hallway much longer, the class behind him would descend once more into chaos. Sarah was wearing a man's flannel shirt that was too big for her. Its sleeves were rolled up past her elbows. "Ever consider peer-tutoring?"

Sarah squinted. "Does it count?"

David was pretty sure that it didn't. But he did know that the principal had the power to waive requirements and alter course codes. It was a common practice to help essentials kids graduate. "I could talk to Mr. Whitcomb."

David looked back over his shoulder. Amos was out of his seat and wandering.

He indicated the classroom with a toss of his thumb. "If you're up to it."

Sarah's eyes darted up and to the left. She was considering it. "Well?"

Her smile was lopsided.

When Nat was almost four years old, David and Anne took her clothes shopping at Wal-Mart. David hated Wal-Mart. But Anne considered it a necessary evil. She was due in two weeks and would be without full salary for a year.

Nat was an easy child most of the time. The two joked years later that Matty was revenge for their first, even-tempered child. She slept through the night after only three weeks. She was not one to cry. She was quiet and introverted and shy. At daycare, she was a star.

But that afternoon, under the constant glare of fluorescent lights—dressed in snow pants from the waist down—Nat was cranky. She was seated in the cart with her legs dangling, and she wanted out. David tried to placate her with tickling as Anne pushed through the racks of bargain clothing. Even he could feel the fatigue in his knees. His eyes were salty and starved of oxygen.

Nat progressed from chanting to kicking. And then she managed to slip the boot from her right foot and propel it into the aisle. There was no stopping her afterward.

David finally cracked after the boot crashed into an elderly woman's cart.

He yanked his daughter from the basket and placed her on the ground. Immediately she sat on her bum in a pout. David and Anne continued to browse.

Minutes later, Anne realized that she was no longer with them. David patrolled the shelves and circular stands. After a while he began to call her name. Ploughing through the circular garment racks, he stared into the clothes, but found nothing.

Anne was on the verge of contacting store security when they heard her giggling. She was deep in one of the racks, clinging to the metal support post.

David had never been so angry with her. Anne joined in the scolding until Nat finally relented and began to cry.

Then something out of the ordinary happened.

"I want to go back," she wailed, between sobs.

"What?"

"I want to do it over."

David looked at Anne, but her face offered nothing in return. "We're going home," he told her.

"No," she shouted. "I want to do it over." And then she fought her way past David to the cart.

He was too stunned to stop her.

Nat's face was red with heat and frustration. Her pale hair, drawn into short pigtails, was at odds with the seething concentration in her face. "I ... want ... to ... go ... back."

"What is she doing?" Anne's voice was high. She bent to collect her.

"No." Using both hands, Nat pushed the cart back down the aisle, dragging shirts and pants off their hangers as she snagged them on the way past. Other shoppers glanced over surreptitiously.

David stood out of the way.

Nat did not stop until the cart was resting in the place it had been before the argument had erupted. The spot where she lost her first boot.

"I want to do it again."

And then David understood. "Nat," he said. "We can't go back. What's done is done."

"This isn't normal," said Anne, behind him.

"I want to do it over."

David could see that Nat was sorry and exhausted. The hair around her face was wet with perspiration and tears. She was experiencing regret for the first time.

He lifted her back into the cart.

"David," said Anne, "we can't play into this. It isn't right."

She was probably right. Anne was frequently right. But he didn't know what else to do.

Nat sighed, stifling a sob, and placed both hands on the cart handle.

David looked at Anne. "Just push."

Nat was an angel for the rest of the day.

Anne's tongue was swollen and glued to the roof of her mouth. Her brain felt loose in her head. If she moved it would rattle in her skull. Light was leaking into the room from the half-drawn blinds. Her eyes hurt whether she opened them or kept them shut. She was both sweaty and cold beneath the heavy comforter of her hotel bed. And she could not draw the sheets high enough to cover her bare shoulders. In the walls, vague and distant, she could hear the rush of water.

She swallowed down the first wave of nausea and lay still. Slowly she began to take in the corners of the room.

The rally had been an enormous success. The late edition of the CBC tossed out the number 100,000. And she did not doubt it. People. Students mostly. Had come from all provinces to march in solidarity with the No campaign.

There had been champagne later. Too much champagne.

She met the Minister's wife for the first time. Anne did not understand that she would be there at the rally. But it was fine. Gabe left the celebrations early. Returned to his suite with Lana and their kids.

But not Anne.

She loosely remembered arguing with Danny Cummings, who was also drinking. They were loud and obnoxious and they were entertaining the other Liberal party members with their show. And after a while it actually became a joke. They were doing it for laughs the way she and David used to at staff gatherings and dinner parties.

It was fun.

And then some of them took a cab to Ste Catherine Street. To a nightclub. They danced and danced. Like she hadn't danced since university. Danny Cummings danced, too. And bought her coloured drinks with sweet flavours. The club was cavernous. The ceiling was a distant rumour lost above steel rafters and strobes. There were mirrors and ante-rooms and catwalks and staircases that went god-knows-where.

She remembered requesting Abba and then "Staying Alive" by the Bee Gees. "Dancing Queen" was her favourite song, even if it was cheesy and David hated it. Anne hadn't felt so free in years. Certainly not since Nat. At one point, in the bathroom, she looked at herself in the mirror—past the dishevelled hair, smeared lipstick, and running mascara—and thought she was beautiful.

Her eye flickered there in the bed, the moment she thought of her daughter. Then she remembered that she had not called Matty to wish him good night. Her throat made a sound and again she was forced to fight down the acid in her stomach.

"What did you say?"

The sleepy voice of Danny Cummings came like a slap. He rolled over in bed and placed his cold fingers on the flesh of her exposed shoulder.

Anne reached out and opened the drawer to the night table. Just in time.

She promptly puked.

It was Friday afternoon and the class was full. David was not one to fool himself. The boys had shown up to be near Sarah, and the girls had arrived to evaluate the competition. Even Jessica Number Two was on hand, leaning in the doorway with her head sandwiched between a pair of studio-style headphones. In a pair of oversized high tops, spandex tights, and tank top—for a change—she looked like a cartoon character or the caricature of a Bratz doll. But at least she was here.

He had designed the phony stock certificates on the computer and Sarah had run them off over lunch, so that he had at least a hundred copies of each. He had decided that his students were going to experience the Stock Market Crash of 1929.

The day before he had struggled through a lesson on investment and shareholders. He'd provided the kids with fake balance sheets and gone over concepts like dividends and credit and buying on margin. By the end of the period, he was actually sweating. But he thought that maybe they had a tenuous grasp on it. At least some of it. Who was he fooling? Today was likely to be a disaster and then Sarah, who thought of him as a hero since he'd sprung her from Rebecca's class on Monday, would see him for the failure he truly was. Or had become.

"Tamara and Charles will be our brokers, then," said David.

Charles had been absent the day before, but he was one of the brighter kids—hampered more by attitude than ability. Unlike Amos, for instance, he could add and subtract. David could tell that he resented being in a class with some of the slower kids. It was the main reason he skipped so often.

On the chalkboard, David had three stock prices for AT&T, FOMOCO, and Flalans—a dummy land development company from Florida. It was going cheap, and David anticipated that it would be a popular choice among his students. If they bit, the whole exercise would be a demonstration of the underlying problems in deregulation and speculation. Words that he had, wisely, not used in the previous day's lesson.

Sarah had been trained in advance to help the kids maintain their balance sheets. She was enthusiastic and helpful and great with the students. In the few days since her arrival, the class had been transformed.

"Once I ring the bell, trading may begin."

Leonard edged forward in his seat. He was actually excited. Amos stared analytically through his thick cloudy lenses at the blank balance sheet as though it held some secret key.

David raised the old school bell he had brought in especially for today.

"Wait. I don't have a sheet."

He paused. The entire room did. It was Jessica Number Two. Sarah scurried over to David's desk and then set her up with the others.

"Is that Dusty Rose?" asked Sarah as Jessica settled into a chair.

The girl nodded slowly, staring upward under hooded eyes.

"I have the same shade. But it looks better on you."

Jessica smiled.

David rang the bell dumbly. Would miracles never cease?

Throughout the first hour of class, he slowly raised and lowered the price of the stocks. Conservatively with Ford and the telephone company. But by contrast, Flalans skyrocketed from one dollar at the opening of trading, to just under one hundred dollars. All of the kids bought on margin, accumulating huge debts.

At one point, in the heat of the game, Sarah sidled up close to David and whispered, "Aren't they cute?"

David cocked his head. He didn't know what or who she was referring to.

Sarah hit him with the back of her hand. "Amos and Michele," she sighed.

He looked closer at the desk mates. Amos drew something on Michele's paper and she bumped him with her shoulder.

"They're in love," said Sarah.

"Come on!" shouted Leonard. "Post a dividend or something. I'm dying here."

David wrote one dollar on the board under FOMOCO.

"Ahhh."

The other students laughed.

Jessica Pohlman leaned over his balance sheet. "Is that a negative number?"

He withdrew the page. "Shut up."

Now, thought David, with only minutes left in class. And carefully, relentlessly, he began to pull the plug on each of the stocks. A few of the students caught on and dumped their shares, amassing losses nonetheless.

"What are you doing? You bought it for more than that. 'Buy low, sell high,' remember?"

"Yeah, but look how low it is."

David watched the confusion on Leonard's face closely. He was licking his lips and rocking back and forth in his chair. Some students stood and approached the brokers only to stop midway and return to their seats.

"Sarah," some of them called, hoping for advice. "What should I do?"

And she played it beautifully—simply shrugging, and walking away coyly.

"Ahh. You can't do that now."

AT&T and Ford had lost half their peak value. Flalans was a penny stock. Tamara and Charles had never been busier as they pounded on calculators, liquidating their classmates' shares.

David reached for the bell amidst the turmoil. When it rang, the students were stunned.

"That's it?" said Amos. "It's over?"

"You mean that we can't sell anymore?" asked Jessica Pohlman.

"Are we playing, Monday?" asked Leonard. "I'm, like, totally broke. Worse than broke."

"Me too," said a boy named Peter Munroe.

"Not me."

The entire class turned toward Jessica Number Two.

"How can you not be broke?"

"Let me see."

Jessica leaned back in her chair, offering up her balance sheet to anyone interested. She stretched, cat-like.

"You barely bought anything," observed Leonard.

"I barely had any money. It's stupid to spend money you don't have."

David swooped in to discuss the fallout. He told them about Wall Street and the chaos of trading. He talked about overproduction and speculation and foreclosures and breadlines. A third of the country out of work by 1933. The students were quiet, attentive. Desperate to make sense of it all.

And then the bell rang to end class. The kids rose unhurriedly, deliberately, and filed toward the door.

"That was cool," said Leonard. "We should do that again."

Sarah paused by Jessica Number Two. "I guess you're the smart one today, huh?"

And for a moment, David allowed himself to smile.

David was watching a movie with his wife. They had lost all track of time. Matty was asleep at last. Down for the afternoon, he hoped. It had taken two bottles. They were losing it. The fragile threads that held their lives together were unravelling.

Anne hadn't slept a wink the night before. Matty had colic. On the sofa, she resembled an asylum patient, at mid-afternoon dressed in a robe and staring blankly at the screen. Twice already she'd lolled off during the film. David had taken over in the morning, warming bottles, rocking and burping their son. And now they both needed a break.

Upstairs, Nat played quietly with her *toutous*—her word for the collection of plush toys that threatened to engulf her room.

Halfway through the film they heard her on the stairs. Thumping a bit like her mother, taking them one at a time, placing both feet carefully on each tread before attempting the next. The basement stairwell scared her. David had forgotten about her completely. He lived most days in a fog since Matty's birth.

"Hey baby," said Anne as Nat rounded the corner into the family room.

From the corner of his eye, David could see that his daughter had paused in the doorway.

"What's up?"

"Do you like it?" Her little voice sounded like a squeaky toy.

David turned his head slowly. Warily.

"Oh my god," breathed Anne.

David squinted into the dark end of the room.

Anne spoke deliberately, suddenly wide awake. "Don't freak."

Nat was nine months old before she had hair. And even then it wasn't more than a pale downy duvet. At five she had just enough to collect behind her head in some semblance of a pony tail.

David stood, knocking the control—which had been in his lap—to the floor.

"David. Don't."

He couldn't believe it. Her bangs were cropped within an inch of her hairline. The curly lock in front of her ear was gone. He had loved that soft whorl.

"I cut my hair." Her smile was unsure. She had gathered her arms behind her back.

"David," Anne warned again.

But he was already moving past his daughter and taking the stairs two at a time. He couldn't look at her. He wasn't even sure why. She was just so perfect. And now she wasn't. It was irrational, but he couldn't be trusted in that moment.

He found the kitchen scissors beside the sink in the bathroom.

Blond hair littered the floor. He scooped it into his hands. It was soft and light and ephemeral. It could have been feathers or dandelion fluff. She would need a haircut now. Her first ever. To minimize the damage. And it would be short and ugly. He knew already that he was overreacting. But he could not go back.

He could not undo what was done.

Anne fluttered about the kitchen like a trapped bird. She opened cupboards and then shut them again. The water she placed on the stove began to boil. Unconsciously, she tapped the pot handle, and spun, searching for a sign. Her eye told her to touch the pot again.

Matty looked at her. "Aren't we having spaghetti?"

"Spaghetti. That's right." Anne bent and retrieved the noodles from under the counter. The bag, already opened, spilled onto the floor. She gathered the sticks of dried pasta, and then involuntarily she began to tap them on the counter until they were a perfect bundle again. She couldn't help herself, even though she knew the perfect bundle would disappear into the chaos of boiling water only seconds later.

She swallowed and exhaled. "Did you have a good day at school?"

Matty nodded, but did not look up. His tongue stuck out in concentration as he worked with a coloured pencil. He had her father's wavy hair. Anne worried that, like her father, Matty would one day go bald.

Her eye twitched.

She was having trouble looking directly at her son since her return. "Whatcha working on?"

"A drawing."

"Can I see?"

"It's not done yet."

Anne poured the noodles into the boiling water and then turned down the temperature on the burner slightly. She tried not to think of the slow disintegration of the perfect bundle.

She had called in sick on Monday. A first for her.

"Papa makes spaghetti with meat."

Anne fumbled the can opener. It clattered on the counter and slipped to the floor. She bent to retrieve it.

The message on the phone said that David was staying late to mark papers, but that he'd be back in time for supper. Anne figured that he was taking a circuitous route home through one of the bars downtown. Two years ago, Anne might not have questioned the message. Things change.

The can opener would not bite into the tin. She'd wanted an electric one forever.

"Are you making it with meat?"

Anne placed the opener on the counter and leaned forward on her arms. She looked out the kitchen window to the yard. "No, sweetie. I'm just using tomato sauce."

Matty did not answer.

It was November, but early, and no snow had fallen yet. But the yard looked desolate and barren. The shoots from the day lilies were a yellow-brown. She had not yet cut them. Even the hostas, which looked like wilted cabbage, had not been pruned back. The late stretch of summer had finally given way to fall. Her eye twitched again.

Tomorrow was Saturday. She would garden then.

Seeing Danny had not been so bad. The Minister had returned to Newfoundland for a few days, so the office was relaxed. Danny took over in his absence and was gone most days to meetings on the Hill.

Still, he had invited her to lunch, and she had accepted.

"*Maman.*"

The water for the noodles was overflowing, hissing and

seeping yellow rings on the surface of the stove around the burner, like a cartographer's lake.

Anne lowered the temperature further and prepared a pot for the sauce.

Her intent had been to clear the air. She was married. It was obviously a mistake. They could barely tolerate each other on a good day. She half expected to be let down easy by Danny and was prepared to be dutifully indignant but ultimately generous and high-minded.

"You probably know that I've liked you for a long time."

Anne cleared her throat and pretended to choke on a mouthful of white wine.

"Are you okay?" Danny was unsettlingly solicitous.

"Waiter, could we get some water?"

Anne patted her mouth with a napkin. The restaurant seemed suddenly intimate, hanging on their every word.

When she set it down, he reached across the table and held her hand. She placed her free hand over her eye to conceal the pulsing, and then leaned on her elbow, which gave off the impression that she was gazing pensively at the clasp of his hand over hers.

"This must be confusing for you."

Matty looked up from his drawing. "What's an 'understatement'?"

Anne covered her mouth. "Did I just say that out loud?"

Matty stared at his mother. "You said, 'That's an understatement.'"

"Just finish your drawing, sweetie."

"I am."

"Oh, can I see it now?" Anne's voice cracked almost imperceptibly. She buried her face in her apron, and then counted to five.

Everything is going to be all right.

Anne walked around the counter to look over Matty's shoulder.

"Do you like it?"

Anne squinted and leaned forward. There was liquid in her eyes. "It has beautiful colours. What is it?"

Matty leaned on his fist and frowned. "You can't tell?"

Anne scrambled. "Yes. Yes. Of course I can. These are fish, right?"

"Mm hmm." Matty sat up, placated, and pointed. "And that is a seahorse."

"Oh, my."

"And there is a crab."

Anne swallowed hard. "Is this you?"

In the bottom corner amidst the fish was a stick figure with a large head. Its eyes looked like giant goggles.

"No, *Maman*. I can't breathe under water. That's my sister. She lives there now."

David sat across from Sarah in the little classroom. She was helping him mark the multiple-choice section of a quiz he had given. He was working on papers from his European Revolutions class.

It was only five o'clock, but the halls were deserted. Downstairs in the gym the boys would be playing basketball, but upstairs, they were the only people, other than the custodian.

David could hear him in the next room beyond the blinds.

"They did really well."

Sarah was exaggerating slightly. But even David was surprised after the results from the second unit. At least no one had failed this time. And the real star was Jessica Number Two.

"We should take them on a field trip."

David laughed.

"Seriously."

He laid down his pencil.

"But no one takes these kids on field trips."

"There's a reason for that."

"What?"

David leaned back in his chair and looked around the room for the answer. All he saw was peeling paint and poorly illustrated posters of World War I weaponry. The heating system ticked. He had not had a drink all day. In fact, he had not taken a drink during the school day all week. "Things are just settling down. Let's not get carried away."

"But they're hands-on learners. You said so yourself. Maybe a trip is exactly what they need."

David hated being defeated by his own logic. Sarah was right. No one took the essentials kids on field trips. Managing them in the safety of a traditional classroom was already a challenge. No one wanted to be held responsible for them in the world at large. Even if they might benefit. All it took was one student to blow a trip out of the water.

"We could go to the war museum."

"Give them access to weapons?"

The corners of Sarah's mouth turned upward.

David leaned back. He was going to regret this. "Ever been to the Diefenbunker?"

She lowered her lids.

"Now that's a field trip. Prime Minister Diefenbaker built it in 1959 at the height of atomic paranoia. It was to house the government in case of a nuclear attack."

"No 'Stop, Drop, and Roll'?"

"This was just a more expensive version of the same thing. It wouldn't have worked."

"They'd love it!"

"Probably."

A long pause ensued. "Okay, I'll look into it."

Sarah clapped her hands. Then they stood almost simultane-ously. Outside it was dark already. The time had changed.

"Where do you live?"

"George Street."

"Do you drive?"

Sarah chuckled. "Yeah. A Cadillac."

David grinned. "Need a lift?"

"I can walk."

"It's below zero. It's dark. And you live on the other side of town. If all you have is that flimsy coat I saw you with, then I'm driving."

Sarah stared at the floor as David locked the door. "Okay, but I'll have to stop at my locker."

"I'll meet you out back. At the library doors."

There was no hard and fast rule about driving students, but many teachers avoided the practice. The liability was prohibitive.

David was surprised to find the door to the history office unlocked. He was even more surprised to find Rebecca Beames at her desk. Even seated she was tall and severe and her dark hair was pulled back into a bun. She wore a stylish long black cardigan for warmth. Hunched over her desk, she appeared to David like a sinister crow.

She looked up from her laptop, but just a glance, before returning to her screen.

David entered the room and stowed his tests in a drawer.

"You're here late."

"I could say the same." Rebecca did not bother to look up this time. "How's your pet working out?"

She had been pouting ever since David had arranged for Sarah to drop her class. Albeit difficult to notice any real change in her habitual bitter demeanour.

"If you mean Sarah, she's actually working wonders. The kids love her. Especially the boys."

"You'd know."

David recovered his coat from the back of his chair. "What are you implying?"

"I'm sure I don't know what you're talking about." At that, she reached up and collapsed the screen of her computer. "I'm meeting someone for supper."

Poor sod, thought David. He pulled on his gloves and left the room, rather than bite further. You couldn't make some people happy. For weeks, Rebecca did nothing but complain about Sarah's performance in her class. But now that he'd removed the problem, she took it personally.

David waved to one of the custodians before veering left into the library hall. Sarah awaited him at the far end. Indeed, she was wearing the flimsy blue coat. No hat. Hands jammed in her pockets.

David clapped his gloves together as he let the Civic warm. Sarah sat in the passenger seat wrapped in her own arms.

"Safe to say that winter has arrived. Maybe time to break out the parka, huh?"

Sarah just shivered and folded her chin into the collar of her coat. "My mom's supposed to take me shopping on payday."

Inwardly, David winced. He knew better than to make comments like that. Students could be situationally stupid. They could lack forethought. But in this community they could also simply lack money.

David put the car in gear. "Where does your mom work?"

"The chemical plant. She does shift work. She's a cleaner there."

"How about your dad?" David slowed at the east end of the school as someone pushed through the doors. A tall dark crow. He braked.

Rebecca Beames passed in front of the car and glanced left. Another step and she paused and stared into the vehicle.

Fuck, David thought.

One side of Rebecca's lips lifted into a smirk. And then she waved at Sarah. Well, thought David, he'd finally made her happy. Her dinner date could thank him later.

Sarah mumbled something, but David missed it.

He pulled away faster than necessary. "What did you say?"

"I said that woman hates me."

"No. Before that. And I'm not sure that it's you she hates."

"My dad doesn't live with us. He's out west in Fort McMurray. We don't hear from him much."

"Why doesn't she like you?"

David shrugged, and then turned onto the main thoroughfare and crossed in front of the school. "Maybe because you like me."

It didn't sound right when David said it. He wanted it back. And a silence descended over the two as the car shuttled them past a series of gas stations and then onto the highway overpass and into the older part of town. David now regretted his offer. He shouldn't be alone with Sarah. He certainly shouldn't be driving her home at night. Even if it was only five thirty. And now Rebecca had seen him. Seen them.

He pulled onto Sarah's street, which was narrow and dark. A few homes bled blue light from their television screens, but there were no street lamps. The pavement was uneven, and he had to slow in order to negotiate the parked cars on either side. A pickup was on blocks in the front yard of a clapboard row house. The water tower loomed in the near distance.

Sarah broke the silence. "It's the little green one on the right."

The windows of the house were blackened. It looked depressed. He began to put the pieces together. Sarah's two jobs. The insubstantial coat. Single mom.

David piloted the car up on the curb and put it in park. A mongrel dog sniffed about the street in front of them. It squatted to take a shit.

At the far end of the road a group of boys played hockey. Their voices were just audible in the silence of the vehicle.

"Mom's gone till eleven, at least."

David's ears filled with the sound of water. Their arms were almost touching in the tiny cab.

"Do you—I mean, you could … if you wanted to. Come in." She was not looking at him as she said this.

This was his fault. He'd misled her with some gesture. Or maybe he had imagined such a possibility and brought it into being. And now she had never looked younger or more vulnerable to him. The slender neck with its exaggerated tendons. The wisps of hair at her temples. The long fingers, nails chewed to the quick, playing with the zipper of her coat. Nervously rubbing it between her thumb and forefinger.

So close to adulthood, and so far away. An awkwardness his own daughter would never attain. Was that what he saw in Sarah?

"I'd better go."

"Yeah." Sarah's voice lifted, almost cheerful. But when she tried to open the door it was locked.

David fumbled for the release. Too quickly. And then she was gone, walking hastily up the drive like a foal on legs too long for her body.

He rolled down the passenger window and shouted, "See you tomorrow."

Sarah paused with the screen door opened between them. She raised her left hand into a half-wave and pulled it down as though scalded. Then she disappeared into the house.

Anne accepted a second lunch date with Danny weeks later. He and the Minister had flown to China and then to Japan and finally back to Vancouver. With the unity question put to bed, the entire political wing of the Ministry had once again turned its attention toward fish.

Danny sent her e-mails almost every day he was away. He attached photographs to each of them. Boats in Hainan Harbour. Pigeons in Tiananmen Square. The Farmers' Market in Gastown. The photographs were not personal in any way, other than that they had nothing to do with her role in the department. And they were beautiful. There were no captions and no explanations. They bore no relation to his messages. They just were. And he was sharing them. With her.

Anne had no prior idea that he was a photographer. She had never cared to find out.

"He's going to leave federal politics."

Anne blinked, and then blinked again. She did it to cover the twitch. It had reared its ugly head the moment she read Philly Cheese Steak on the menu. She ordered salad. No wine. Just water.

"His wife wants him back at home. Besides, he'll never make PM in this environment. You wouldn't want to anyway."

Anne chewed a leaf of lettuce until it was completely liquefied. Danny had ordered prime rib.

She took a sip of her water. The twitch told her to swallow five times and just before she set it down, it asked for a sixth. She thought she might cry.

"Are you hearing what I'm saying?" Danny sliced into his beef, releasing a slurry of blood and fat into the roasted potatoes. He speared a piece and fed it into his mouth. Before he was through chewing, he added another piece.

"It's over," he said through the food. Danny wiped juice from the corner of his lips with the back of his hand. Anne noticed that he did not switch hands after cutting. David ate the same way.

"It's his wife. Lana just didn't sign on for this. She wants him to help raise the kids. And let's face it. He could write his own ticket on Bay Street now."

Anne picked at a crouton. She willed it to be prime rib.

"You know what this means?"

She nodded. She had no clue.

"A by-election." Danny paused, letting the news sink in. "I'm going to run."

Matty's nose had been running this morning. She might have to stay home with him tomorrow if it developed into something. Two teenagers had died last week from meningitis. It was all over the news.

He's going to be all right. Everything's going to be fine.

"I wanted you to be the first to know. Gabe's behind me all the way."

Danny laid down his utensils and reached for her hand like he had before. That's when she noticed the speck of food on his tie.

"I'll have to go back to Newfoundland, of course. For a little while. But in the end, this can only be good for us."

It was meat. Her eye twitched perceptibly. Danny raised an eyebrow, cocked his head to one side. That's when Anne reached forward and brushed away the morsel. It left an oily stain in its wake.

Danny looked down, and then at Anne. He smiled. His eyes moistened at the tenderness of her gesture.

Anne smiled in return. It allowed her to cover for the incessant pulsing in her eye.

"Let's go back to my apartment."

Anne cleared her throat. It sounded like, "Mmhmm."

Natalie was born by caesarean. Anne was two weeks late and the doctor, fearful of her rising blood pressure, insisted on an induction. David took a photograph of Anne leaving the house at 10:00 in the morning. It would be their last day as a solitary couple. Only it wasn't. The induction was a disaster. Anne spent four days in labour and never dilated beyond three centimetres.

On the fourth day, she finally relented and accepted a shot of Demerol. David returned to the hospital room and lay down on the bed. They had been playing bilingual Scrabble and Anne was killing him. A half hour later, David was shaken awake by an irate nurse.

"How can you sleep while your wife is in labour?"

He considered protesting, but instead rolled quietly to a sitting position.

"The doctor needs you in the other room."

He followed Nurse Ratched—as he'd newly dubbed her—back down the hall to the delivery room where his wife was still swimming in the throes of Demerol.

"We have a monitor on the baby's head," said the doctor. "And everything is fine."

The monitor had been installed earlier that same evening. Unfortunately, the spring-like contraption that was meant to catch in the skin of the baby's head had been originally attached to Anne's cervix. It was not long after that his wife gave up on stoicism and accepted the drugs.

Anne slurred, "They want to perform a c-section."

"Okay," David responded. He was functioning on a half-hour's sleep. He hadn't been to work in four days. He was sweaty and cold, with the itchings of a decent beard.

Anne, for her part, had almost murdered the obstetrician following the cervix debacle.

"We just don't know how much more stress the baby can take."

There were seven women on the ward, other than Anne. All seven had arrived after her. All seven had their babies already.

"I only have one condition," she said. "I want to be awake when it happens."

The doctor laughed quietly. "I'll see what your anaesthetist says when he gets here."

Anne gripped his lab coat.

The doctor's expression changed.

Her voice cut through the Demerol haze. "I didn't spend ninety-six hours in labour to miss this moment."

"Right."

David scrubbed in and was allowed to watch. Anne asked for a play-by-play.

"It doesn't look real," he said.

The doctor had his hand buried in Anne's lower abdomen.

David was so entranced that he almost forgot to raise the camera when Natalie was pulled out.

"It's a girl."

Only, after four days in the birth canal, Nat looked like an alien with her elongated head. She was purple-green and trailing afterbirth.

Dumbly, David stared into the viewfinder and snapped the shot.

Anne was crying.

Nurse Ratched moved in close to David. "Don't worry. Her head will come around in the next few days."

On his way home for a shower, David turned on the windshield wipers. Then he started giggling uncontrollably. It wasn't raining. He couldn't see for the tears in his eyes.

But after he had wiped them away and settled into his drive, a strange thought occurred to him. It came unbidden and surprised him after years without the slightest consideration. Was this how his own father had felt? And if so, how did he ever leave?

Paul Whitcomb offered to offset the cost of the bus with money from the Coke machines. Permission forms were sent home, lost, and sent home again. When they didn't come back, David called home. He left messages. He called again, until finally, after two weeks of trying, all thirteen students were cleared for take-off.

The timing of the trip could not have been better. The class was wrapping up Canada's involvement in World War II and entering the Cold War era, in which the Diefenbunker was built. David could not gauge just how much the students were taking away from the class, but at the very least they were attending and enjoying themselves. No one had set any fires. And clearly, Sarah had been correct in her analysis of Amos and Michele. They elected to sit together on the bus ride to Ottawa. They were, indeed, in love.

Sarah, for her part, showed up every day and worked her magic on the boys and Jessica Number Two—in whom she had developed an acolyte. David watched as the two girls sat side by side on the bus, sharing a pair of headphones and smiling at what they heard.

At the Diefenbunker, a young university student boarded the bus to speak with the class. She was a tad over-jovial and obviously had a script from which she did not stray, but the kids were good and attentive. They were the last tour of the season. The bunker would close for the winter the very next day.

"Bring your coats," the guide warned. "You'll find the blast tunnel to be very cold."

David allowed the kids to disembark and then joined them at the tunnel entrance. From the surface, the Diefenbunker appeared to be nothing more than an oversized septic tank buried in a farmer's field. But immediately upon entering it took on a completely different vibe. It reminded David of spy films or the opening sequence of *Get Smart*.

The tunnel, built like a large corrugated iron culvert sloped gently into the earth, was lined with thick, mysterious cabling.

Twice during the descent the guide stopped to explain some point about the construction, and the existence of two model weapons—one a nuclear missile, the other a replica of Fat Man, the bomb that levelled Nagasaki.

"We learned about that," Leonard piped up.

A small pang of pride resounded through David. What a motley crew they must have seemed to the guide. Sarah turned and smiled. It was the first personal exchange they'd shared since he'd driven her home. At last, it was a sign that the two could reconnect. Each period they shared had crackled with awkward restraint. But if the kids noticed, no one said anything.

In his departmental office, all civil communication between him and Rebecca had ceased entirely.

"The first station we'll see once we pass through these doors will be a decontamination chamber."

Even the name sounded menacing.

"Look at those doors," said Jessica Pohlman.

"Cool. It's like we're entering a bank safe."

The guide smiled. "You haven't seen anything yet. Wait until you see the vault downstairs where the nation's gold would have been stored."

The kids wandered wide-eyed through the complex. They laughed at the technology of rotary phones and fat-panelled televisions. They marvelled at the complexity of the boiler room, and stayed far too long fighting over the ancient Nintendo control for their chance to play Russian Attack.

The facility had everything from cafeterias and barracks to dental surgeries and a radio broadcast room for the CBC. A few of the students had brought pocket money and agonized over what to purchase in the gift shop. Amos eventually decided upon freeze-dried ice cream, which he promptly split with Michele. Jessica Number Two bought a pair of earrings in the shape of the Avro Arrow. And Sarah lent Leonard—who had no money—enough to purchase X-ray glasses.

"Don't look at me with those things on," Tamara warned.

However, the most popular items by far were the Cold War shot glasses featuring the likeness of Nikita Khrushchev banging his shoe at the United Nations.

David stopped Sarah before they entered the bus. "This was a great idea."

She blushed. "I didn't even know this place existed."

"I mean taking the kids on a trip."

She shrugged. "It's a day off school for me too." And then she skipped up the steps.

David felt something vaguely familiar as he stood in the chill afternoon air. It occurred to him that it just might be happiness.

There was a photograph of Natalie holding a stray cat. A slim calico that wandered into their backyard late one evening when Nat was seven years old. It was skittish and aloof and kept to the fence line whenever anyone stood on the back deck to coax it over.

Anne mixed bits of bread with milk so that Nat could entice it with food. Her daughter was determined—jaw set like a plumb line. It was late summer. The sun had already drifted below the maple crowns that backed onto their yard, angling dappled and burnt amber through the thick foliage. Anne watched her daughter in the gloom. Crouched and gently calling. The girl's patience was foreign to her. She loved all animals with an intensity that bordered on violence. The way a mother loved her children.

At her birthday the year before, a little boy had tried to crush a spider in their basement. Nat fought him off with her hands, knocking his cone-shaped party hat askew and bringing him to the brink of tears. While Anne frantically tried to calm the guest, Nat cupped the tiny creature and freed him in the hedge along their walkway.

When the cat refused her overtures and the offering of milk, Nat marched to her mother in the kitchen and demanded sandwich meats.

"It's almost dark, sweetie. Maybe you could try again tomorrow."

Armed with mock chicken, Nat sat cross-legged and humming in the damp grass. The molly paced a short distance off, arching its back and calling in a broken voice. It was rail-thin and mottled. The light had almost gone from the sky when it finally slunk over and ate from Nat's outstretched hand.

Her daughter looked back at that moment, and Anne was there to catch the triumph and the joy. The same look she captured in the photo—Nat's toothless smile.

For a season and a half the old girl lived beneath their deck, eating dry pellets and leftovers outside the patio doors. Over winter she became pregnant, and Nat tended to her every day after school, no matter what the weather. Anne could still recall the shushing of her snowsuit as she trooped across the kitchen.

But a freak storm in March rocked their home the night before Nat's first piano recital. Anne fretted through the night, pacing and reading. In the morning she was haggard.

She found them beneath the back deck in a box of straw and blankets Natalie had prepared—five dark question marks, and no sign of the mother.

Nat played "Twinkle Twinkle Little Star" in the recital that morning, brimming with anticipation of something that would never come to pass.

Dallas Desaulniers arrived two and a half months late for class. He was a lanky seventeen-year-old parading among kids two years younger than him. He had dark hair and deep brown eyes.

He glared at the room from under the brim of a Yankees base-ball cap, set slightly off-kilter. With high cheekbones and a wide mouth, he looked vaguely native. He wore a camouflage hunting jacket and ripped jeans. The steel-toed boots on his feet were either two sizes too large, or he was descended from a family of genetically gifted clowns. His walk was loose-limbed and men-acing, as though at any moment he might snatch your wallet and make a run for it.

David stood from where he had been bowed over helping Amos. Sarah turned to watch him enter, too. He was handsome in a roguish sort of way. Jack Nicholson in *One Flew Over the Cuckoo's Nest*.

"Can I help you?"

"Is this history for retards?" He stared down the dozen other students who were spaced out at the computers and scattered around the island of desks. "'Cause I've gotta good feeling about this. Three times a charm, right?"

"Do you go to this school?"

"I do now." He passed David a wrinkled timetable. "But I'll be absent tomorrow."

"Oh?"

"Court date." He winked at Sarah.

David noted that indeed Dallas had been added to the class. "What school are you coming from?"

"The Falls. My mom doesn't want me no more, I guess. So I'm here now with my dad."

"Well, you can take a seat. Sarah, can you get Dallas a copy of the assignment?"

"Dallas?" Charles snickered.

"You wanna eat lunch through a straw?"

"Okay. Okay. That's enough, Charles."

Sarah had to pass next to the boy to reach David's desk. Dal-las followed her with his eyes.

David demanded his attention. "Did you take history in the Falls?"

"I think so."

"You don't know?"

"I kicked the shit outta some kid and they gave me twenty days. Didn't see the point in going back after that."

"Airtight logic."

"Are you always this funny?"

One of the boys laughed. Probably Charles. A short burst through his nose. It might have been Peter Munroe. They were seated together behind David.

"Why have you elected to grace *us* with your presence?"

"Probation. And my dad would probably kick my ass if I missed the first day."

Sarah handed Dallas the photocopied paper. He looked her directly in the eye before finally raising his hand to receive it.

"We'll get you some notes together for tomorrow."

"What's she staring at?"

Michele looked away and then to the floor, the way she always did when she was uncomfortable.

Amos spoke up. "Leave her alone." He pushed his thick glasses back on his nose.

"What are you gonna do about it?"

"That's enough, Dallas. Amos, I'll handle this. Get back to your work."

Dallas opened up into a broad grin. It was obvious to David that he had a talent for exploiting frailty. "Oh. Is that your girlfriend?"

The other students laughed. This only encouraged him.

"You tapping that?"

"Dallas."

"So Amos is a player." Dallas raised his hand for a high five.

Amos slumped into his chair and stared morosely at nothing.

"That's enough."

Dallas stood up from the table, pouncing backward, feline and agile. His hands were raised in mock surrender. "Okay. Okay."

Sarah said something beneath her breath.

"What's that?"

"I said, 'Big man. Picking on kids half your size.'"

It occurred to David that the two were probably the same age. The chronology of authority that Sarah held over the others did not exist with Dallas.

"I think you should sit down."

Dallas spun and stood facing David, less than an arm-length away. They were almost the same height. "Who asked you to think?"

The room went quiet as though someone had let the air out. He closed the small gap with a half step.

David braced himself.

Then Dallas sprang backward again and clapped his hands. Sarah took a step away, startled. David hoped that the students had not seen him flinch. "Just kiddin. You can all relax now."

He pulled out a chair for himself and then threw his big boots up on the seat of another.

After class David walked to Whitcomb's office and entered without knocking. Rebecca Beames was sitting demurely in the visitor's chair with her legs crossed.

Paul arched his eyebrows and leaned back. "David?"

"Sorry. Can we talk about this new kid?"

Whitcomb raised his hands and pointed in Rebecca's direction.

"It's okay, Paul. I have to go anyway." Rebecca smiled as she passed David on the way out.

David shut the door. "Paul? Since when are you two on a first-name basis?"

Whitcomb shrugged and sighed. "Your ears must have been burning."

David ignored him. "What's this about adding a kid to my essentials class almost three months in?"

Paul leaned forward. "His dad brought him this morning. Guy's a truck driver. Not the kind of guy you'd want to meet in a dark alley, by the way."

"No warning. Nothing. Shows up halfway through the period and causes all kinds of hell. You know what these classes are like. You can't just drop a bomb in there."

"We can't exactly turn the kid away either. The dad's headed to Florida tomorrow. Supposed to be on the road two weeks. We needed to expedite."

David collapsed into the chair where Rebecca had been only moments before.

"For what it's worth, I'm glad you came to see me. You've been doing great things with those kids." Paul folded his hands together on the desk in front of him.

David could sense the conversation was about to shift. "What?"

He shrugged, and then came clean. "Rebecca says you gave the Evans girl a lift home the other night."

David could hear the sound of running water. Just a trickle. "That was like … two weeks ago."

"You think that was a good idea?"

A tone sounded in the hallways, and was followed by an announcement. David could not make it out through the walls.

"What are you trying to say? And why is she in here talking about it now?"

"Come on, David. Don't be obtuse. You bend over backward to have the girl sprung from Rebecca's class. We make her a special spot in yours. She's practically joined to you at the hip, now. You take field trips together. And now you're taking her home? Do the parents know?"

"Know what? I drove her home, Paul. Do I need a union rep?"

His principal waved his hands above his head. "Okay. Time out."

But David was already standing. Adrenalin was coursing through him. And his ears were full of the sound of rushing water over stones. A cataract of white noise. He couldn't control himself.

"David, sit down. We're just two friends talking here. How's Anne?"

David leaned forward. "As one friend to another, fuck you."

Matty's school was a Catholic school. A French Catholic School. This meant that they still celebrated Christmas. Not "the Holidays," but the actual "away-in-a-manger-baby-Jesus Christmas." This meant pageants.

The school gymnasium was packed. Only the worst parents did not attend the Christmas pageant. There were more video cameras per capita than in a Japanese tour bus.

Anne and David had not been out together in months. And yet here they were, crammed into plastic chairs only inches apart, smiling to people they used to call friends and sweating in their winter coats.

Last night the first snow fell, and Matty had worn his new snow pants to school for the first time. And earlier in the week his teacher had the class write letters to Santa. The children were supposed to turn the letters over to their parents following the show.

The room rolled with the din of a hundred different conversations. And at the front, a music teacher scurried back and forth between the band and her own upright piano. Naomi Clegg was her name, and she used to give private lessons to Nat every Thursday at lunch hour. She was very strict, Anne remembered. If a student failed to bring her books, Mrs. Clegg refused to teach the lesson. And you forfeited your twenty-five dollars. David raged over this the first time it happened. And on each subsequent occasion as well. Nonetheless, he smiled profusely upon crossing her in the front foyer earlier and wished her a Merry Christmas. But that was David. The consummate gentleman. Full of pent-up anger and passive aggression.

Anne had spent the afternoon with Danny. The Minister had been back a week, but the House was closed for the holidays and their disappearance was not too conspicuous. She was trying to avoid close quarters with her husband. As she always did on days with Danny. She was worried that he could somehow discern the infidelity through smell or pheromones. Her eye twitched and her face flushed just thinking about how close David was to her now.

The man on Anne's right looked at her expectantly. Had she said something?

Anne turned and smiled. The man nodded. The edge of his lip rose slightly in return.

Beside her, David sat slouched and scowling and silent. Anne suspected problems at school.

"What number is he on the programme?"

Startled into life, David opened the photocopied brochure and scrutinized it in the half-light of the gym. He sighed. "Last. Of course."

Before leaving home, he confirmed with her that they would leave immediately following Matty's performance. Christmas used to be David's favourite time of year. Anne recalled his midnight antics. Upon waking the children, he would encourage them to hasten to the living room, where they would huddle and jockey for a space by the picture window to watch Rudolph's nose as it flew into the night. Behind them, David would wave a laser pointer over the trees in the park beyond the next street.

"I see it," Nat would croak in her night-time voice.

And Matty would sully the window with his fingers as he craned for a better view.

The evening consisted mainly of carolling, with the odd student-written play—"How Santa Got His Elves," "Frosty's Magic Hat." Anne was convinced that David dozed off more than once. She nudged him as the second-last number came to a close.

This was the big one. The nativity scene. Matty was the Third Wise Man. He would be bearing myrrh. When the information slip came home, it said that parents were responsible for providing the appropriate costume. Anne purchased a used bathrobe from the local Goodwill, onto which she hot-glued gold brocade. David fashioned a crown from the top of a pizza box and covered it in tin foil.

"What's 'myrrh'?" asked Matty.

"Good question," said David.

In the end, Anne gave Matty a small jewellery box he could present to Jesus.

Mary and Joseph entered as a narrator explained their quest for a room. Anne held up her camera. There was an almost constant throbbing pulse in her eye as the story progressed and Matty's moment drew closer.

"What did you say?" David whispered.

God. What did she say?

Everything is going to be fine. Matty will be perfect.

Then he was there. Anne spotted it immediately. Matty, or the teacher, had not properly attached his robe. The belt had only one loop, and it dragged dangerously by his feet.

Anne was groaning. Low, but perceptibly.

"Are you all right?"

Matty made it to the manger without incident. He said his line. Or at least his lips moved. Anne could not hear over her own moaning.

The crowd began to chuckle. Matty stopped. He hadn't

turned over the myrrh. It was still in his hands. Anne could see his little mind working. He could forget about the gift and take his place in the tableau, or he could go back, drop it off quickly, and fix the problem.

The narrator paused.

Matty looked at the box in his hands and shoved it into his robe. Only to do so, he had to crouch over and lift the flap, and then tuck it up under his belt. The crowd roared as Matty squatted and scrunched up his face in concentration. It looked as though he were finishing up on the toilet.

Anne feared mental scarring.

Finally, he joined the shepherds and the other Wise Men. As the narrator approached the end, the kids began to file off the stage.

Matty tripped over his belt. By itself, it would have been fine. Passed unnoticed. But the box came loose, hit the stage, and popped out the back of the robe as he progressed. It looked to the audience as though her son had just laid an egg.

The crowd cheered.

Anne kept the camera in front of her face to cover the twitch in her eye.

"Well," said David. "That wasn't so bad."

Later, in the car, Matty waved goodbye to a female classmate. Anne helped him into the rear seat.

"Did you see me?" he asked, once they were all inside.

"We sure did," David replied.

"I forgot to give Jesus the myrrh."

Anne could see his big round eyes when she looked into the back. "Did you?"

"I was afraid you'd see."

David pulled away from the lot.

"*Maman?*"

"Yes, sweetie."

"I think I lost your box."

"That's okay, baby."

"I have my letter for Santa."

"Can I see?"

Matty handed the folded paper over the seat. It was decorated in red scribbles and green blobs. Anne opened it. As David passed under a street light, the letter cleared. There was only one request.

Anne folded the list.

David looked at her quickly. "What's it say?"

Anne stared out her window. "He wants us to be happy."

David did not speak to Anne on the drive to Paul Whitcomb's house. The fragile world of Room 219 was slowly unravelling. It weighed on him. He had already been drinking before she arrived home, and intuitively Anne took the seat behind the wheel without being asked.

They had not yet discussed her behaviour at the pageant two nights ago. Nor had either of them commented on Matty's wish list. For his part, David was presiding over the sacking of Rome. In many ways, Dallas Desaulniers was more effective than any Vandal or Visigoth. Unlike those fifth-century tribes who chipped away at the edges of civilization, Dallas infiltrated the city itself and corrupted the vital systems that sustained it. He was the lead in the plumbing.

Anne pulled the car up to the curb just down the street. Many staff members had already arrived. David could see Melinda pushing up the laneway with her husband in tow. She had a wine bottle tucked under her arm. It was wrapped in a bow. David looked at Anne, but she was busy unbuckling her belt. Before they left home she asked, "Are you sure we shouldn't bring a gift?"

David made a noise in his throat.

"I was just asking."

If she saw the gift-wrapped wine bottle, he wouldn't hear the end of it.

Anne had arrived late this evening. But this had become increasingly normal. David assumed that it had something to do with Minister Caulie's surprise announcement. David had pegged the man as a future prime minister. He supposed, though, that the politician's new position as a consultant at a Toronto law firm was a more lucrative move.

As he watched Anne exit the vehicle, it occurred to David that they had not even discussed that either.

In fact, of late, their only exchange of particular note had transpired just before leaving home this evening. And it had to do with Sarah.

The sitter they normally used had not been available and, floundering for another, David decided to call Sarah. The girl's mother dropped her off just as Anne was pulling into the drive.

Later, as Anne was stepping from the shower and then searching through her closet, she asked, "So Sarah's a student?"

David could tell, despite his wife's restraint—in waiting until after her shower—and in the flippant manner of her asking, that the question was loaded.

"Not exactly. She's a peer helper."

Anne allowed a suitable time to elapse.

"She's very pretty."

"Is she?"

"Come on, David."

At that moment, it occurred to him that the awkward invitation he had received from Sarah the month before had probably been a result of the way other people perceived her. She would always be a sexual object first—to both men and women. And her reaction to this was to fulfill that image. Somehow, the two of them had moved beyond this—and now offered each other something the other needed. Something outside immediate expectations. But as he looked at his wife, he realized just how far the gap had opened between them and that he could never explain the thing that he barely understood himself.

As they had earlier in the week at the pageant, David and Anne arrived as a united front. Paul answered the door, cheeks flushed pink, forehead moist at the hairline. He, too, had already been drinking. For a moment, his smile wavered as his eyes fell on David. But it only took him a second to recover, extending his hands toward Anne.

The way they grasped each other—as though they were about to play London Bridge—hit David like cold water. He recalled the same embrace the afternoon he lost Nat—between his wife and the woman beside them on the beach. Sometimes it happened that way. Without warning.

David pushed his way into the foyer. After kicking off his boots, he made his way up a flight of stairs to the kitchen. Christmas at the Whitcombs' was the closest thing to a tradition that David adhered to. He knew the house intimately after years of staff parties, Super Bowl get-togethers, and year-end basketball bashes. All of which involved alcohol.

They had been good friends. In truth, Paul might have been David's last friend. And now even that was up in the air.

At the top of the stairs he confronted Clint Martel, the Co-op teacher. Clint was a sailor in his spare time, counting the days until retirement and a life on the inland waterway between his slip on the St. Lawrence and his new condo in Florida. Increasingly grey-haired and bearded, Clint was the quintessential "old man and the sea."

Les Aaron was standing next to him—slender and pasty and handsome against all odds.

David nodded to both men.

Les was the art teacher who had offered to give him scuba lessons years ago. They too had been friends once.

"David. We hardly see you anymore," said Les.

Clint quietly nursed his beer.

"You made any headway on the book? I'm telling you, man. Divers come from all over the world to explore those wrecks."

"Still in the planning stages," David lied.

"Strike while the iron's hot, my friend." Les had his hand on David's shoulder, but was addressing Clint. "This guy. I tell you. Sitting on a gold mine."

Les had any number of irons in the fire at one time. Public murals, bronze sculptures, a hand in the design of a new Maritime Centre planned on the city's waterfront. David had once thought and acted just like him. It was probably the basis of their friendship. Now David was no more than flotsam on Les's current.

He attempted to switch the focus to Clint. "Do you dive?"

But Clint just pursed his lips and shook his grey head. "I stay on top of the water, if I can help it."

Les turned away and began picking at the label on his beer bottle. That he might have been insensitive in his choice of words did not register with Clint.

David pressed on. "When's the big day?"

"Well, I can go in May. But of course, I'll see out the semester. You can bet the boat will be packed and waiting for July first."

David envied the conviction Clint held in his plan. He, himself, could no longer see past next week. Planning had, of course, been proven overrated in David's estimation.

Les touched David's arm. "I gotta bend that guy's ear about an idea I have. Good to see you, David. Get yourself a beer, man. Relax."

Awkwardly, David hung on with Clint, but neither man could think of anything to say. Chris Morgan became his unlikely rescuer. Chris was a few years younger than David, but he was the school's social worker. He had short spiked hair and a diamond stud in his left ear. He wore torn designer jeans and a v-neck T-shirt that flaunted the shape he was in.

"David! You don't answer my e-mails?"

Clint drifted into the living room without excusing himself.

"Sorry, Chris. It's been a rough week."

"I've been meaning to connect with you regarding Dallas Desaulniers. See if he's okay."

"Oh? You should drop by the class sometime."

Chris smiled as though David had just told a good joke. In truth, David didn't really know the extent of Chris's role in the school. He often saw him standing in the smoking area on the front sidewalk of the school, sharing a laugh with the kids. They didn't address him as Mr. Morgan, but as Chris. He did not know the man well, as Chris had come on staff the fall after Nat's death. And mostly David had walked through that year like a zombie. He was, perhaps, a little jealous of the younger man's rapport with the kids. But then he'd had something akin to that himself once.

"Kid's had it rough, you know."

"That right? I'd say he gives as good as he gets, then."

Chris offered up the same smile, but pressed on. "Dad's okay. But he's a trucker, eh. Never home. Can't stand mom. Drug addict. You know how it is."

David did know, sort of. But he wasn't feeling particularly generous. "How's his assault case?"

Chris looked as though David had slapped him. "Yeah. Well. It doesn't look good."

David remained silent, expecting the full story. Knowing Chris couldn't help but share the gossip.

"Guess he beat up some developmentally delayed kid at his old school."

David allowed his head to roll back, incredulous.

"The kid wasn't retarded or anything."

"Oh, that's good." If David had expected irony, it wasn't forthcoming.

"He played football up there, or something. Dallas had a habit of heckling him during games. Even showed up at practices."

David thought about the boy's treatment of Amos. Earlier today, Dallas had blown a kiss at Michele just to get a rise out of him.

"Anyway, you know the saying, 'Bigger they are—.' Guess he jumped the guy at a party. Beat him bad."

David perched on the corner of the kitchen table. "And you want to make sure he's okay?"

Anne's voice rang clear from the next room. She was telling a story.

"Well, yeah. Is he?"

David was not one to count his wife's drinks, but when she went up in decibels, he knew she'd had enough. Consciously, he stuck to Coke and later to coffee. For once, he actually didn't want to drink, anyway. He was vaguely aware of Rebecca Beames's late arrival, but the party was well attended, and Paul's house was large. Avoiding her was easy.

Around midnight, David managed to pry Anne away from Les, of all people, and help her to the car. He fished through her purse for the keys. She sat in the passenger seat, semi-conscious. He hadn't seen her like this in a long time.

At home, David paid Sarah and went to the kitchen for water. "Uh, do you need a lift?"

"No thanks. I called my mom."

"Probably a good idea."

David wasn't sure, but he thought she was smiling in the dark hallway. A moment later, headlights flashed over the ceiling.

"I think she's here."

After hanging up his coat, David went to turn out the lights in the kitchen. He was surprised to find his wife awake. She was sitting at the counter, staring at a picture Matty drew on the refrigerator. She was unsteady on the stool where she sat.

"You okay?"

She swung her head, trying to focus on David. "Know what that is?"

David shoved his hands in his pockets and touched Anne's keys. "It's late. You've had a lot to drink."

Anne blew air through her nose. "*You're* telling *me* that *I've* had too much?"

"Before I forget." David tossed his wife's keys on the counter. "I'm going to bed."

Anne slapped them to the floor with the back of her hand. They came to rest at David's feet.

Calmly he bent to retrieve them. "Did you get a new house key?"

Anne made a choking sound.

David peered at her. "What's wrong with your eye?"

Anne held out her hand for the keys.

David closed his fist around them. "What's wrong with you?"

"The same thing that's wrong with you. The same thing that's always wrong."

David swallowed and hung his head. "I'm not doing this now."

"Of course not. Do you love me?"

The question caught him off guard. "Don't be ridiculous." David turned to leave.

"You were sleeping when it happened."

He stopped. All around him the room filled with water. "What did you say?"

"I know you blame me. That you've always blamed me. But you were sleeping."

She was an ugly drunk. And in that moment David was revolted by her. "It was your turn to watch her. I left her with you for half an hour, and you lost her."

"She just went to rinse herself!" Anne's voice was a high-pitched whine.

He'd hurt her. And to his dismay, it felt good. "And she didn't come back, Anne."

"I know she didn't come back, David. I check her room every night while you're sleeping, hoping it's all a terrible dream. And knowing—knowing that it's not."

David pitched the keys into the sink, where they clattered against the metal basin. It was juvenile, but it made him feel better.

She bit her lip and sat straighter. "It's not my key." Her voice was suddenly cold and empty.

"What?"

"It belongs to Danny Cummings." Anne allowed him a second to digest. "It's the key to his apartment, and I think I'm leaving you."

Leonard missed two days in a row at the end of the last week. David had not seen Jessica Number Two since the previous Monday, except for a moment when she appeared at the doorway, saw that Jessica Pohlman was also absent, and then took off.

Today, David had just over half a class. Amos and Michele, of course. And then five others. He looked at the empty room and then at Sarah, who was braiding Michele's hair in anticipation of the bell to begin class.

David had a terrible kink in his neck from having slept on the sofa all weekend. And his eyes were strained from the fluorescent light. He was mildly hung over, but slowly recovering. The first two periods had been worse.

Dallas, whose attendance had been perfect—but for court dates—had not yet arrived. But David dared not hope. Attendance was part of his probation. And if anyone knew where the line was and how to push it without going over, Dallas was the man. He would drift in two minutes late just to prove that it was he who was in control—in case anyone was wondering.

The anger David harboured all weekend had been supplanted by a strange levity. An odd sensation of freedom. He could almost feel himself letting go of things. Like a juggler who no longer cared whether the balls continued to spin. Perversely, he almost wanted to witness what it would be like to watch them fall.

In the beginning, the Jessicas were sure to show up. Their interest in Dallas went beyond academics. But according to Sarah, he made out with one of them at a party. This in turn caused a rift in their friendship. The following weekend, he made out with the other. And now the two were re-banded in shared hatred and unlikely to show up for class. Staying away conveniently being their preferred method of protest.

During that same period of time, Dallas had managed to lure Leonard into his confidence. David had seen them together more than once on the sidewalk at the front of the school smoking cigarettes. In addition, Dallas had secured himself an ally during his daily campaign to undermine David in the classroom. Leonard's recent disappearance mystified him. In fact, he was completely surprised at just how much the boy's betrayal hurt him.

The bell rang.

"Okay. Today we're going to talk about the October Crisis. Michele, could you get the textbooks and help Sarah distribute them?"

David did not feel much like teaching. He had a documentary on the edge of his desk, and planned to stick it in the VCR as soon as possible. It was old and in black and white. The kids would hate it.

"Whoa." Dallas stalled in the doorway. "This place is deserted." He had an extra-large coffee in his hands.

David was, at least, relieved to see Leonard skulking in behind the older boy. He did not look David in the eye.

"Must be the flu or something." Dallas took a sip of his coffee and strolled around the room, considering the most advantageous seat from which to mount his assault.

Amos sank into his chair and tried to appear invisible.

David turned to grab two more textbooks from the shelf, but as he did so, from the corner of his eye, he saw Dallas brush past Sarah and lightly tap her buttocks.

Sarah spun in response. "Fuck off, pig."

David swallowed. His jaw was sealed tight and flexing.

Dallas moved cautiously in pantomime around Sarah, not turning his back. "Did you hear that language?" His eyes sparkled.

Leonard stood frozen with the back of a chair still in his hand. He looked from Dallas to Sarah and then to David.

"You will apologize to her." David tried to sound nonchalant, professional. But even he thought it sounded like a threat.

Michele looked at the floor and patted her newly formed braids.

"Or what?" Dallas did not respond well to threats.

This was the moment when David was supposed to find exactly the right thing to say to defuse the situation. And deep down, he probably knew what that thing was. He suddenly just didn't care.

"You know damn well what."

Sarah attempted to step between them. Leonard seemed frozen in time. And like earthworms drawn upward by the light of a full moon, the Jessicas arrived in tandem at the door.

Dallas broke the spell momentarily with a smirk. "Oh, I get it. Amos ain't the only player here." He looked back and forth, visually connecting David to Sarah. "Mr. Henry, you dog."

In the room, no one batted an eye. The water was almost over David's head.

"You ought to be ashamed. She's young enough to be your daughter."

It was not precisely the punch of a heavyweight champion. In truth, it was a bit too slow and landed only as a glancing blow. Had Dallas not been so thoroughly surprised, he might have sidestepped it entirely. But to David's eternal satisfaction, it still managed to set the little punk stumbling backward onto his ass. The coffee crashed over the floor.

And although David might have imagined it, he was convinced the boy had begun to cry. But by then, David was halfway down the hall and on his way to Paul Whitcomb's office. To turn in his keys.

The House on Water Street

David helped the child count out his change. Bits of lint and what appeared to be the remnants of a Kinder Egg toy were scattered among the coins.

"You're short a nickel." He watched the child's shoulders slump. He looked at the empty penny dish. "Don't worry about it."

The boy scooped the pile of candy and gummies into his hands. "Thanks, mister."

It was Sunday morning. Slow. Vermaelen's Dairy did not often experience a rush, but Sundays were David's favourite shifts. He could start a book at six o'clock in the morning and have it done by day's end. He preferred detective fiction— Inspector Rebus or Kurt Wallander. He had grown particularly fond of the compressor hum of the refrigerators. After ten years behind the counter, he could often predict the exact moment it would clatter into life.

If he ran short of books, David could simply grab a magazine from the ample rack. Vermaelen's claim to fame—if it had one—was its magazine selection. It covered the entire east wall of the store, floor to ceiling, and you used a rolling ladder to reach the upper shelves. Vermaelen's had everything from *Seventeen* to *Working With Wood* and *Guitar World* to the *Christian Science Monitor*. In fact, it was the only store to carry many of the more obscure subscriptions. But this niche was a well-known secret and drew residents from across the city.

Many customers came just for the reading material, and probably never realized that they could nab their milk and cat food as well.

The store was shaped like a shipping container with the front door at one end and the register at the other. Chest-high shelving units, running the length of the store, divided up the floor space. Coolers and refrigerators on the right. Magazines on the left. It hadn't changed in forty years. David sat on a stool behind the register, ensconced in a fortress of cigarette packages and lottery tickets. Splayed on the counter was an issue of *Model Railroader*. He was currently reading a review of Hornby's new Flight of the Mallard train set bundle. He'd discovered the magazine here one evening years earlier after he'd read everything else of interest, including an article from *Cosmo* promising "101 ways to please your man." *Cosmo* was a guilty pleasure. But not for the articles.

At first the world of model railroading appeared foreign and quaint. Its very existence in the twenty-first century seemed an anomaly. But more and more often he would pull down new issues, until the journal became one whose delivery he anticipated. He fell in love with the trains, the stations, and the tiny worlds people created. It all seemed so safe and contained and self-sufficient. And there was a beauty to the mechanical workings. The careful, detailed paint jobs. It seemed to David that function had lost its form in the modern world, but here there was still art.

Tomas Vermaelen had hired David after a series of short-lived jobs as a painter, a security guard, and a disastrous stint as a barista at Starbucks.

"You are a teacher?" The old man was still slender, if a bit stoop-shouldered and pigeon-chested. His hair was thin, white, and receding. But his most memorable feature was his great hooked nose.

"Was."

"You think perhaps you are overqualified to work in my store?"

"You'd be surprised by the limited skill set of a history teacher."

"You are funny." The man did not laugh. "A sense of humour is good." Vermaelen had immigrated to Canada from Belgium in 1967, and he spoke with an accent. Although he was Belgian and Flemish, he dressed like a Parisian labourer in dark blue monos. "The last kid I hired, I caught screwing his pimply-faced girlfriend in the stockroom. This too was amusing. Do you have a girlfriend?"

Vermaelen lived above the store, but at seventy, he was ready to relinquish the daily grind. David always assumed that the old man gave him the position based on the fact that he did not have a girlfriend.

Vermaelen's had a fortuitous corner lot location on an otherwise unfashionable street. It was one part local grocery and convenience store, one part smoke shop, and one part unlikely magazine hub. The magazines were an accident of fate, according to Vermaelen.

"It started with the Vietnamese in the 1970s," he said. "They were looking for copies of papers from Saigon. After that, it was the Lebanese in the eighties. And pretty soon you had the Bosnians and the Somalis making inquiries. People just kept asking, 'Can you find me this?' 'Can you order that?' Word got around.

Sure, I said. You need a litre of milk too? How about the lotto?"
He smiled. "Tell me, David. Why are you spending your life
ringing in Pepperettes and Joe Louis?"

He could have fought it, of course. The union rep told him
as much.

"Consider your family, David. Your pension."

But after David recovered from the initial shock of his
actions, he felt relieved. Buoyant, even. He walked away consciously with his eyes open. He had to hand it to Whitcomb,
though. In spite of everything that had passed between them,
he'd talked down the Desaulniers boy's father. He'd come to the
school looking for a lynching. David never knew precisely what
his friend had said or done or promised. But whatever it was, it
worked.

He'd even been the one to help David find a new place to live.
The house on Water Street was a rental belonging to a retired
colleague and principal in the neighbouring school board. It was
in the heart of a university town on the shore of Lake Ontario.
Just large enough for David to disappear into. Anonymously.

At first, he saw Matty every other weekend, but within a year
Anne sold the house and moved closer to Ottawa. A small bedroom community off Highway 7. And visits fell off into irregu-
larity and then to special occasions.

"What's all the metal shit in his face?" Vermaelen asked
David during Matty's last visit. "He must really piss off security
at the airport. Does he have a girlfriend?"

The boy maintained a bedroom at the house on Water Street,
but, like David's life, it was devoid of personality—no posters, no
colour on the walls. When Matty visited, like hotel guests, they
inhabited the same space, and saw each other only in passing.

The roller skates were an afterthought. David bought them on clearance. They were light blue and mauve and made of plastic. For her real birthday present Nat was receiving a toy horse with plush fur. It whinnied and tossed its head and even played the theme song to *The Lone Ranger*.

In the end, it was the roller skates that carried the day. David parked the car at the end of the driveway to block off a roller rink. Nat spent the whole next day on it. Coming in only for meals. The skates were adjustable and slid over her running shoes. Their plastic wheels were ill constructed and required real effort to gain forward motion. And the mechanism that locked them in place was faulty and slipped regularly, necessitating frequent correction.

But none of that mattered to Nat. All day David listened to the scratching of the plastic wheels over asphalt. The skates would gather speed until Nat reached the extent of her rink, or the skate slipped, requiring David's attention.

When she concentrated, Nat had a habit of sticking her tongue in the corner of her mouth. As she practised the side-to-side motion of skating, her tongue traced an opposing trajectory, like the pendulum of a clock. She came in for supper smiling through chapped lips. Tiny red cracks, vivid and raw.

Anne sat outside the principal's office, legs crossed, tossing her foot. The secretary looked up and offered her a sympathetic face. Her name was Caroline, and she was good at the sympathetic face. Anne knew this because she had often been on the receiving end of her practised smile, which was really an inverted frown.

Anne smiled back and imagined scratching out the woman's eyes with her long red nails.

"Anne." Principal Kirkland was a tall, athletic man who competed in triathlons. He was ten years older than Anne, but could have been the same age. Sadly, they operated on a first-name basis.

"Hi, Allen." Anne extended her hand and he took it in his, and then cupped it with the other. He was a good principal. He'd have made a good politician, too.

He knew better than to offer her the sympathetic face. Instead, he looked her in the eye with his lips clenched into a tight line. "Sorry to bring you in like this, again." He stepped to the side and, with a wave of his hand, ushered her forward into his office.

Aside from diplomas, the walls were covered in team photos and inspirational posters. Under a rowing team at dawn, one read "Together we achieve more." Anne sat without needing to be invited.

"Did Caroline fill you in?"

"I didn't actually speak with her," Anne replied. "Our receptionist took the call. I was in a meeting." Anne was Acting Director of Communications at the Department of Fisheries and Oceans. When Danny wasn't at his constituency office in Corner Brook, they drove into the city together. He was a backbencher in the opposition party, but ambitious and sat on many different parliamentary committees.

Anne's job was an arm's length from the new minister—a Conservative whom Danny despised. It made for difficult dinner conversation.

"Matt went to English class stoned."

Anne's eye did not move. She took an excellent pharmaceutical cocktail of select serotonin "re-uptake" inhibitors that employed fluvoxamine and citalopram with a hint of buspirone, to be sure. But it still whispered to her quietly from time to time. Only now it said, *Everything is going to be fine. We can get through this.*

"Are you sure? I mean, where did he get the drugs?"

Allen broke protocol with a sympathetic face. But this time she deserved it.

"What's the punishment?"

"Five days."

"Not three?"

Allen shook his head. "Not this time."

"But what about exams? It's already June."

"His teachers tell me that he's not in danger of failing anything. His lack of motivation frustrates them. But ultimately, he doesn't have to work very hard to pass. Count your blessings."

When Matty was in grade seven, a French teacher recommended him for testing. His grades were slipping. "I think he's gifted," she said.

"Really?" It was not what she expected to hear.

"I don't think he's being challenged."

His IQ, according to the WISC III, placed him in the top two percentile.

"His Verbal scores were hampered by the arithmetic a little, but his Performance scores were off the charts," the psychologist said.

Every year thereafter, the school board sent him to Carleton University for two-week enrichment courses in May—Mystery and Myth, How to Be a Dictator, or The Anthropology of Science Fiction. This year, he refused to go.

It seemed to Anne that every time he came home now, Matty had sprouted another piercing—in his nose, his eyebrows, different locations on his ears. She wasn't sure, but last week, Anne thought she noticed an odd-shaped lump under Matty's T-shirt, where his nipple should be.

She bought his clothes. She signed his permission papers and made his appointments. She fed him supper at night and gave him pocket money for lunch. When he wanted a cellphone, she bought him a cellphone. In addition, she at least tried to open the lines of communication. In spite of all this, he was drifting away from her by increments. Like the ice caps, he was shedding his edges and retreating inward toward a centre that was reduced and remote.

At the door to the front office, Allen took Anne's hand the same way that he had in greeting. From the corner of her eye, Anne saw Caroline offering up the sympathetic face. She squeezed. Allen would perceive the gesture differently than it was intended.

Llewellyn Purcell was their leader. Their guru. The grandmaster of the model railroad. The fact that he was fifty, unwed, and lived with his mother, was an unfortunate cliché. David eventually got over it. He wasn't sure that it was ever an issue or concern for the other members of the Frontenac Model Railroad Club. It was completely unlike David to join anything—let alone a group of grown men who dedicated large portions of their lives, and finances, to building models. But he had noticed a short ad in the classified section of *Model Railroader* one Sunday afternoon—two or three lines of text only—reminding all and sundry of the next meeting of the Frontenac Model Railroad Club. New members always welcome. The address was within walking distance of the house on Water Street. His curiosity got the best of him.

"Did everyone bring their Goldenrod?" Llewellyn held court on Thursday nights, from six thirty until nine thirty, in order to accommodate the members who worked during the day. Llewellyn, or Lou, as they called him, did not work. He had been an Anglican minister in a past life. But nobody was quite sure why he left the cloth. Or if they were, no one talked to David about it.

"Almost every minister I know or knew was a model railroader," he once said over a beer at the Village Idiot. "A man can only have so much faith, I guess. He's got to have control over something."

Control. Whether David wanted to admit it or not, this was part of his draw toward model railroading.

David spaced out his dried sprigs of the weed as Lou had. Sometimes the group just sat around and talked. Sometimes they operated Lou's layout. But tonight was a class on deciduous-tree-making for HO-scale railroads.

"Start by snapping off the tops," Lou commanded. "If you leave these on, the end product will look like something out of Dr. Seuss." Lou was an unassuming man. He was of average height, but dumpy with a preference for flannel shirts. His hair was thin and wispy and, under the fluorescent bulbs of his mother's garage, his scalp shone through the pale strands. He wore solid-framed glasses that were out of fashion before they were sold.

"Now strip the stems down like so, until you're satisfied with the architecture." Lou held the specimen up for inspection.

The others did the same.

Tonight there were four members in attendance, including David. Two of the men he knew only in passing—a father and son. But Dirk Müller was a regular who pre-dated David in the club. He was an American, originally from Düsseldorf, by way of northern New York.

Dirk operated a near perfect scale model of the D & H Adirondack Branch from Saratoga to North Creek and Sanford Lake. It was an HO scale that ran a late 1970s diesel engine. He had built it with two other club members and opened it to the public once a month.

David had been out there with Lou last year. The layout was housed in a massive metal garage, twenty-five by forty feet. It ran eighty feet along a cantilevered surface around the walls. In total, it had 193 linear feet of track and was so complex that it required at least six men to operate.

Unlike David and the other two men, Dirk was here strictly for the social aspect. This was ironic, in that he was a dour, silent man.

"We're going to use two colours of fine foliage. A light green and a dark. But first we'll spray the tops with a mixture of similarly coloured paint."

Of all club nights, David preferred the seminars and workshops. Model railroading appealed to the historian in him, but working quietly with his hands gave his mind a focus that absorbed him and allowed him to live, however briefly, in the moment. One of the happier memories of his childhood also involved trains. He had once received what he understood now to be an inexpensive train set for his birthday. His father helped him tack it to a piece of plywood on the floor of his room. It was a nondescript model of the Canadian Pacific. A black and red engine made of plastic. David spent hours in that room watching the train pass around and around. When his parents took to arguing, he simply turned up the speed of the little engine and laid his head on the plywood, untreated foundation. Soothed by the clickety-clack.

While the paint dried, Lou took them for a tour of his own layout. David and Dirk were intimately aware of the OO Berwick Upon Tweed railroad. But the father-and-son duo had never seen it run. While significantly smaller than Dirk's behemoth, there was a genius in Lou's creation. A level of detail that bordered upon the obsessive. The simple irregular oblong track form was built upon a cork board ten feet by six feet. The northeastern section was dominated by a stunning viaduct over glasslike resin water and adorned with an island station that was a preternatural replica of the original building. It included a locomotive depot with hand-painted rolling stock, freight sidings, a fiddle yard, and unrivalled natural scenery.

The moment David saw it at his first meeting, he was hooked.

And for several years now, unbeknownst to even Lou—the closest thing to a friend David had—he had been constructing his own layout in the cellar of the house on Water Street.

As the evening progressed, the men brushed the trunks of their deciduous trees a flat grey and then covered the crowns in extra-thick-hold hairspray. They sprinkled their creations in fine foliage and set them in Styrofoam to cure.

David would stop by after work tomorrow to gather his vegetation. It was his intent to install them over the weekend.

"What do you do with all the stuff you make here?" Lou asked him over a tumbler of Scotch, once the others had left.

"I keep them in the basement."

Lou shrugged and sipped his Glenlivet.

It wasn't exactly a lie.

"Kissy Kissy" by the Kills pounded out of the pickup's speakers and over the quarry. A bonfire stretched twenty feet into the air, sparks and ash floating into the atmosphere. On the far shore in the headlights of half a dozen cars, two girls screeched as they leapt from the rock ledge and into the green phosphorescent water, wearing only underwear.

Matty smiled and looked into the pitch of the night sky as he grooved to the dirty blues hook in Jamie Hince's guitar. In one hand, he held the neck of a half-empty beer bottle. In the other, the end of a spliff.

"Pass it over, fuck."

Darius was too stoned to leave the ground where he lay propped against a washed-out grey log. His girlfriend, Tina, was nestled into the crook of his arm, one bare brown leg thrown over his lap.

The bedrock still held the heat of the sun.

Around them, the party continued to grow until it wasn't just one party, but pockets of interconnected parties dispersed around the square of the quarry. It was still early and still June. And they were all still in school. But it was Friday and it was also hot. Darius nabbed him at the park after school. Tina made room in the cab and climbed into the back with the twenty-four bottles of bootleg beer. Mr. MacDonald had caught a whiff of the pot he and Darius smoked over lunch, and sent him to the office. Matty thought it best to skip the lecture and wait for Darius elsewhere. Now they'd been at the quarry for hours, swimming and drinking and smoking.

Matty relinquished the joint. He was shirtless and barefoot. His jean shorts hung low over his slim hips, almost dry now.

"There's that chick I was telling you about, man."

Matty gazed lazily through the smoke and flames, head still bobbing.

Tina sat up. "What chick?"

"Fuck. It doesn't matter. Just some chick." Darius forced this through the pot he held in his lungs.

She was skinny with short hair. Like Matty, she wore jean shorts and was dancing barefoot. Her arms were outstretched, thumbs in contact with her ring fingers like a meditating Buddha—head lolling between her shoulders. She wore a tie-dyed shirt of red and green and yellow.

Matty stood still.

"Who the fuck is she?" Tina had just noticed her too.

"Ah, shit. Just some chick. Moved into that place across from the funeral home."

"How do you know her?"

Darius sucked on the last embers of their roach. Tina punched him in the stomach.

"Fuck. Jay works with her at the canteen."

"Why haven't I seen her at school? And why were you talking to Matt about her?"

"She's like home-schooled or something."

"You're an asshole."

"No. Really. Her dad's like an engineer. He builds airplanes or some shit. They moved here from Germany."

Matty turned. "She's German?"

"No." Darius looked sorry he ever brought it up. His ball cap was pulled low over his eyes. "They moved back to Canada. She's from Ottawa. She went to the American School of I don't fuckin know, but her dad got some big job back here. They arrived partway through the semester. Now she's doing her shit online."

Darius punched his girlfriend in the shoulder, and she fell back.

"Ow."

Matty could hear them kissing, but he was watching the girl through the fire. The iPod had shuffled and now it was playing the White Stripes through the powerful Bose speakers. Matty didn't know the tune.

"What's her name?"

"Oh, my God. It's like, fuckin Heidi."

"I thought you said she wasn't German."

Darius laughed. "I'm shitting you. I don't know her name."

"You know what her dad does for a living, but you don't know her name?"

"I can't remember. Go ask her."

Matty took a deep breath and blew into his bangs. She was dancing with Jay and another guy he knew, named Rob. He made his way around the fire, weaving through the partygoers.

The music was louder on the far side, but he could still hear snippets of laughter and the screeches of teenage girls across the quarry. Someone dropped a bottle and it smashed by the side of a parked car. The smoke blinded him temporarily and then he was almost upon them.

"Hey."

"Man, fuck. How are you doing?" Jay was polluted. Much

worse than Darius or Matty. He was short but handsome with gelled hair slipping into his eyes. "What did your mom say about the vacation?" Some people said he looked like Johnny Depp. Others said Richard Grieco. Either way, he was *21 Jump Street* through and through. He was also an aficionado of The Cure.

"Don't know. Haven't been home yet."

Rob passed Matty a fresh beer from his cooler. "Did you get suspended again?" How the two ever became friends was a mystery. Unlike Jay, Rob was a redneck—tight jeans, flannel shirt, and steel-toed boots. It was practically a uniform.

Matty took a sip. His heart was beating fast. The girl, still dancing, stared at him through strands of tatty hair. Surreptitiously, he tried to do the same.

"Fuckin guy shows up stoned to MacDonald's class."

The guys were still cackling when she grabbed Matty's left hand and continued to dance. He felt electricity shoot through his pelvis.

Jay laughed. "This is Kim. Kim, Matty. Matty, Kim."

"Hey." Kim grabbed the beer from Matty's other hand and tipped it back until it was gone. He watched her Adam's apple bounce in her throat. Her breasts tight under her shirt. She tossed the empty over her shoulder, and wiped her mouth with the back of her hand.

At the sound of breaking glass, someone yelled "Opah!"

She dragged Matty away from the light to the edge of the quarry without ever letting go of his hand.

"Let's go for a swim."

He was fucked.

Her son's bedroom was forbidden territory. Anne entered anyway. She told herself it was a war. A war she was losing. She needed to go guerilla.

Telling Danny would only bring strife. She'd take care of things before he returned from Ottawa in the morning.

Things had run late on the Hill. He called and told her he would sleep at the apartment. At first, Anne thought the little condo an extravagance, but it was part of his allowance as an MP and it had come in handy tonight. Anne was glad to have it and to have Danny out of the house.

Matty's room was large. He had a queen-sized water bed, a dresser, and a corner wall unit with an L-shaped desk. Otherwise, it was all floor space. At least under the clothing, Anne assumed there was floor space. The door stuck on a hoodie as she pushed it inward.

In her arms, she carried a stack of clean laundry. This was her excuse in case she was caught. She could not believe how much clothing he owned.

Because it was Friday, and Matty was no fool, Anne did not really expect to see him until late. Maybe not before Saturday morning. He would know just how much trouble to expect and, as a result, have taken the path of avoidance to purchase one more night of freedom. Her half a dozen text messages had mysteriously gone unanswered.

The curtains were drawn across the window. Anne waded through and pulled them back. Dust danced in the beams of sunlight. The Danelectro guitar she and Danny had purchased for him for Christmas stood in its cradle like a shrine amongst the general disarray.

Anne's original plan had been to sit down and talk. The women in her fitness class all had teenagers. And they all read self-help books to learn how to deal with them. They would be horrified to learn what she was currently up to. Keep the lines of communication open, they told her. Let him come to you.

But, of course, Matty was out when she came home. No doubt with Darius. And to keep busy, Anne elected to do the laundry. That's when she found the condom. And then the whisper started.

At first, she was surprised. Its faded iridescent package lay at the bottom of the drier, forlorn and forgotten. It doesn't mean that he's having sex, she thought. They hand them out at school. Better to be prepared. But it ate away at her.

She was not aware of any girlfriends. He did not talk about any girlfriends.

Anne pulled open the sock drawer and fished around inside. It was that easy. She withdrew a ball of socks. Inside was a Ziploc bag. The contents looked like Spanish moss or dried oregano. She dug further. Rolling papers. A hand-tooled pipe like something he'd fashioned in shop class.

Her eye pulsed. Not quite a twitch. She took a breath. She counted backwards from ten. Then, she began to empty his drawers onto the floor.

It only took a minute, but the mess was complete. She'd never be able to put things back right.

No condoms. Was this a good thing? Was it bad? Did he need them this evening? Anne moved on to Matty's desk. There was no stopping her. The closet was next.

The cellar in the house on Water Street was just tall enough for David to stand upright. His head grazed the floor struts above. There was a single 100-watt bulb in the middle of the room, but still it wasn't enough. Shadows pooled at the edges of the room. On one end, the stairs met the dark earth floor, and in an alcove stood the oil furnace. At the far end, a greasy yellowed window captured the evening murk. The rest of the room was a railroad. Intricate and incomplete. But already ingenious and beautiful in its geometry.

The last of the spring water was gone. A week earlier, David wore rain boots as he sloshed about the layout. He felt like Noah, fiddling with last-minute preparations.

Like Lou's masterpiece, David's railroad was built on cork board—only it was slightly longer. At twelve by six feet, the diorama took up most of the room, and David had to be careful as he worked his way around either end.

It was constructed of interconnected planes. Upper and lower. It was a scale model of the London-to-Manchester line. As terminals he designed two simplified versions of Euston and Piccadilly stations, with an intermediate stop at Stoke. The upper section, which was Manchester, even had a rolling stock depot.

He'd ordered and built garages, store fronts, double-decker buses, and track-side adverts. There were dry stone walls complete with intermittent hedging. Streets, signage, pedestrians, and power lines. But his crowning achievement was the train itself.

He'd ordered it from Hornby's in England the previous Christmas—an LMS streamlined Coronation class modelled after the City of Chester. It came as a set with three passenger cars, painted in crimson lake with gold and black livery. The most powerful steam engine ever built in Britain. It was obscenely expensive.

But it wasn't what he wanted. Not ultimately. He spent six months researching and sanding and repainting the set in order to recreate an exact copy of the 1937 LMS Coronation Scot—a train originally built to commemorate the coronation of King George VI and Queen Elizabeth. It was the first of the Princess Coronation class trains, and to the best of David's knowledge, it did not yet exist as a scale model kit. This was the sort of thing he had learned model railroaders drooled over. Customizing.

David placed his drill bit against the layout and pierced a small hole. Into this, he dropped Krazy Glue and then planted one of his newly crafted trees.

When David was through with the trees, he tested the train's clearance. It was perfect.

The railroad was now as much a part of the house as its foundation or a wall. It could never leave the cellar unless it was torn apart.

He could never count the hours he spent here. It took him half a year of evenings and weekends just to figure the electrical. In the winter he worked in a coat and scarf. He wore gloves with the fingertips cut away. And when he wasn't here, he was at the library. Examining railway photographs in books and online.

He had decided upon the London-to-Manchester Piccadilly by accident as much as design. He had thought at first about the Canadian Pacific and its passage through the Rockies—a grander version of his childhood set. But it was a matter of capturing the scale of the thing in his tiny cellar. Then he thought about England, birthplace of the locomotive, and the only place he had ever been overseas. On his honeymoon with Anne. After a decade without her, he did not harbour any illusions about recapturing the past. He was simply after symmetry, scale, and the predictability of a static loop. The rest was research.

Next, he would tackle the four arched roofs of the Piccadilly train sheds. It would take months. Maybe more.

Kim's parents gave her the entire third floor of their brownstone home. Her younger sister Chloe hated her for it. It was an apartment unto itself with two separate bedrooms, a bath, and an open concept living space with kitchenette. For whatever reason, it had never been completed and the floors were unfinished plywood. Both bedrooms had exposed lath walls. But otherwise it was a cozy, quiet space.

Oddly, Kim slept in the smaller bedroom, which was no bigger than a closet, on a single-bed mattress on the floor. In the larger room, which looked out on the street through an oval window, she had an art studio. In it, there were two easels and a table with paints and brushes. The floor was covered in drop sheets.

Against one wall, various sizes of canvasses were stacked on a slant. Paintings in various stages of completion.

Kim pulled one back. "This is my favourite."

Matty didn't know what to say. He felt provincial and small.

"Do you like it?"

"Yeah."

"That's it?"

"I … it … you could have your own gallery."

Kim smiled. "You think?"

Matty could never tell if she was being serious or secretly making fun of him. He found it painful to be near her. Worse when he wasn't. She was a year older than him, and once she completed her missing credits online, she'd be done with high school. He had another year to suffer through.

"Marc told me the same thing."

"Who?"

"No one. Just a friend from my old school."

Someone pounded on the attic door. "Can I watch a movie on your TV?"

"No. Go away, Chloe."

"But Dad's watching some stupid documentary."

"Too bad."

Matty could hear the girl thumping back down the stairs.

"You're so lucky you don't have siblings."

Matty bit his lip.

Kim worked at the canteen in Riverside Park. Which mostly meant she sat in a lawn chair sunbathing while Jay made fries. She was tanned deep brown, and her scruffy hair was slowly turning blonde at the tips. The way she wore eye makeup made her look like Angelina Jolie.

"Actually, I had a sister." He didn't know why he said it. He didn't even really remember Nat.

"Oh my god. I'm so sorry."

Matty shrugged and shook his head.

"It was a long time ago. I was like four."

"What happened?"

Matty felt flushed. The apartment was stuffy and warm and smelt like turpentine. He could see through the unbuttoned work shirt down the well of Kim's breasts.

"She drowned when we were on vacation."

Kim placed her hand on Matty's chest. "That's awful."

But Matty thought it was wonderful. He could feel the pad of each fingertip through his T-shirt. The heel of her palm.

"I don't really remember her much. There are pictures, so— I'm not sure whether they're memories or just things I've seen in a book, you know?"

Kim slowly closed her fist, bunching the fabric of his shirt. She pulled him forward.

Matty had to bend down to kiss her—which felt strange. She seemed so much taller in his mind. She tasted like cigarettes and gum.

He was worried she could feel him stiffening through his shorts.

When she stepped back, his head was spinning.

"I really want to paint you," she said.

Matty nodded. "Uh, okay."

"Naked."

Anne glanced down at the screen on her treadmill. It read four kilometres. She imagined each bead of sweat as melting fat. The thought calmed her. One kilometre to go. She thought she might actually die.

On the machine beside her, Camilla was racing. Ponytail. Spandex. Heart-shaped ass.

We're going to get through this.

Bitch.

Camilla had introduced Anne to the world of Isagenix. First as a customer and then as a salesperson.

Originally, Anne envisioned shedding weight while substituting the odd meal with IsaLean shakes and nutrient-rich supplements. But what she ended up with was a diet plan. Cut coffee. Cut wine. Work out more. Take in less fat. Limit breakfast and lunch to 240 calories. Dinner at less than 600. Four hundred if possible.

"Look at you," Camilla used to say each time they met. "I told you this stuff really works."

Camilla had crazy eyes. You could see the whites around the iris at all times. To Anne, the only thing worse than a sympathetic face was someone with crazy eyes. She used to think that the woman was simply high energy, but after a year, Anne wasn't so sure. What she thought was a burgeoning friendship might simply have been an elaborate sales pitch. She wasn't sure where the pitch stopped and the real woman started, or if it was even possible to separate the two any longer.

And yet, here she was running five kilometres on a treadmill with the woman, three times a week at the YMCA on Argyle and O'Connor.

Ever since Anne joined Camilla's team, the compliments had dried up. "Have you done a cleanse this month? Remember, image is everything in this business. No one buys weight loss products from a fat woman."

In reality, Anne had never been in better shape. But she'd also never been more unhappy. She hated running. Hated it.

Nutritional cleansing and detoxification, however, she loved. At least in the beginning. The very words soothed her. But the cost. If Danny only knew what she paid to join Camilla's team. Their heart-to-hearts about weight loss and gaining control of your life had all but dried up now, too. The only thing Camilla wanted to discuss was recruitment and sales.

A tinny alarm sounded and Anne's treadmill slowed to a walk and then, eventually, to a stop.

Camilla tossed a towel around her neck. "Great workout, huh?"

Anne could barely speak. She wanted to curl up in a corner. Instead, she nodded her assent.

Camilla was a walking, talking male fantasy. Tall, trim, blonde, and impossibly big-breasted. Barbie dolls longed to look like her. "Did any of those girls in your office buy in?"

"There are a couple on the fence," Anne managed to squeeze out.

"Well. Bring them over. Reel them in."

Anne towelled her face. "How old is Maya now?"

"Huh? Maya? Oh, seventeen. No. Eighteen."

"Is she sexually active?"

Camilla practically barked with laughter. "What time is it?"

"Four o'clock? Why?"

"Because I make sure not to arrive home before five."

Anne stared blankly. Camilla could have walked out of the Y and into a cocktail dress. She had barely broken a sweat.

The woman leaned in close and whispered, unnecessarily, but for theatrical impact. "So I don't walk in on anything I don't need to see."

"But aren't you worried?"

"Worried? If I were getting it that regularly I wouldn't need to be here three times a week. Let's hit the showers. You look terrible."

When Kim told Matty she was going to host a party, he said, "Cool." When she said it was going to be a lobster dinner party, he shrugged and said, "Sounds cool."

They'd just had sex on the floor of her tiny room. He wasn't sure just how many times they'd actually had sex, because he'd lost count. And at that moment he thought everything sounded cool. And he wasn't sure precisely how you actually counted the number of times a couple had sex, anyway. Did you go by the number of times the man ejaculated, or by the number of orgasms the woman experienced? And how did you know for sure when the woman had an orgasm?

He didn't understand why people left the house when they could be having sex. And he was elated to see that Kim more or less agreed with him.

Of course, she invited Darius and Tina. And Jay and Rob. And when word went around that her parents weren't home, a few other people showed up uninvited.

Kim had never actually cooked lobster on her own, but that was the least of the problems with her party. She thought it would be best to eat late and she set the table in white linen with real silverware. She even pulled up bottles of wine from her dad's wine cellar. She lit candles, even though it was light until nine o'clock.

Her mother was some kind of part-time caterer, or so Matty understood—although he'd never seen her cater anything. But that meant the set-up looked fantastic. Until the guests arrived. Their dining-room table sat twelve comfortably with all the leaves in, so even Chloe and her boyfriend were welcomed to join in.

Originally, Kim was expecting the mysterious Marc and another friend from Ottawa, but for whatever reason, neither of them materialized. Matty couldn't say he was too upset about that. He didn't like how Kim casually dropped his name to justify her opinions on art or life. If he never heard another, "Well, Marc says…" that would be just fine by Matty.

Things started well enough, but went south quickly.

Too much time and access had been allotted to drinking. At the quarry, this was not an issue. In a well-laid dining room, the problems were more glaring.

By the time Kim brought out the lobster, her guests had begun to fling the buns off the end of their forks in an effort to upset their opponents' wine glasses. Jay lit a joint and passed it around the table. Some lanky red-headed kid with a goatee named Raff had 'shrooms. He was rumoured to be a dealer.

Matty had never really seen Kim upset before. It didn't stop her from trying the 'shrooms, though.

"What are you guys doing? This is a dinner party."

People settled for a few minutes as the curiosity of the crustaceans gripped them. But no one really knew how to go about eating them. And Kim managed to find only a single nutcracker. Rob tried to crush his claw under the heel of his shoe. Jay took his outside to smash it on the sidewalk. When it worked, the rest of the assembled guests paraded onto the lawn to do the same.

Matty tried to round them up and bring them back inside, but after a while, it occurred to him that outside was the better place for them. The dining room was a disaster. And so he locked the door.

Kim had already retreated to the attic crying and hallucinating. Matty spotted her fleeing up the back stairs lifting her knees abnormally high.

"What are you doing?" he shouted after her.

"I can't go anywhere without stepping on these fucking Smurfs."

Thoughtfully, Darius and Tina stuck around to help Matty with the mess.

Monday was David's day off.

Actually, Vermaelen was so bored with his semi-retirement that David could realistically have any day he wanted off. Mondays were just sure things.

David walked to the book juggernaut on Princess Street. He needed help with his design of the Manchester Piccadilly train sheds.

His Internet research had turned up numerous photos from fellow enthusiasts, but not much in the way of construction tips or materials. He was hesitant to contact Lou or Dirk without giving away what he was up to.

David preferred the smaller independent bookstore across the street, but he knew they wouldn't have what he wanted in stock. The first floor looked like the houseware section of a department store, peddling scented candles and glassware. Eventually, he found a computer. A few moments later, an overly friendly employee stopped to help him. Her nametag reminded her that her name was "Chaztatee." David assured the girl that he needed no help. He made several jot notes in his ringed pocket pad, and then went in search.

He was surprised to find more than one resource. But then again, he'd been surprised to discover originally a subculture of model railway builders. He tried *Basic Model Railroad Benchwork* by Jeff Wilson first, but it lacked detail and David realized with some satisfaction that he was beyond what the book offered.

Then he looked at *Realistic Model Railroad Design* by Terry Koester. He flipped through the colour plates—recognizing the process he himself had taken with his own layout. He paused at a particularly relevant image.

"Mr. Henry?"

David knew without looking. But, of course, he looked anyway.

Sarah Evans.

She was still tall. And slender. If not a bit fuller. Tanned skin. Or maybe it was the makeup. He did not remember her with makeup.

"Sarah."

Her hair was cut differently. She looked older. But not old. Indeed, she had become beautiful.

David was suddenly keenly aware of his own dishevelment. The dirty jacket and wrinkled T-shirt. The decade-old sandals. Unfashionable shorts.

He sucked in his stomach. Had he shaved? Of course not.

A moment of awkward silence settled in.

"Wow, I can't believe you're here."

David raised a hand, palm up. "I could say the same."

"What are you reading?"

David held the book down by his leg. "Just some hobby stuff. Do you live here?"

"No. I'm based out of Calgary, actually. I'm visiting my mom."

They stared at each other, while searching for something to say.

"And, well, I have friends who went to university out here so I thought I'd shoot over for the day."

"Great."

"Yeah."

"Yeah."

"How are you?"

David opened his mouth. He smiled. "I'm good."

"Good."

"Yeah."

"Yeah." Sarah had an expensive coffee in her hands. Something with whip cream.

"Based?"

"Pardon."

"You said you were 'based' out of Calgary."

"Oh, yeah. I'm a WestJet owner—aka airline stewardess."

"Just what you wanted."

"Yeah."

"Well, you look fantastic."

"Thank you."

David noted with disappointment that she did not return the compliment. Just then, the helpful employee snuck up behind David. "Did you find what you were looking for?"

"What? No. I mean, yes. But it's not what I was looking for. I mean—hoping for."

"Let's take a look. Maybe I can help." She reached for the book in David's hand.

He took a step back. "No." He said it with more vehemence than he intended.

Now the employee felt awkward. Her eyes shot side to side. Time to retreat.

When she was gone, David stuck the book back on the shelf and leaned against the spine casually, blocking it from view.

Sarah smiled. "Oh, I almost forgot. I'm engaged."

"You are?"

"Yeah." She held up the ring.

"Wow."

"Yeah."

David wanted to punch himself out.

"He's a pilot."

"I'm so happy for you."

She continued smiling and nodding.

"Well. I'm supposed to meet my friends upstairs."

"Right. Great."

"I just recognized you and wanted to say thanks."

"Thanks?"

"Yeah."

"Great."

"Yeah. I was pretty messed up when you met me. My dad ... well ... I guess I just never ... what am I saying? I didn't know what it was like to have a father. I was confused, you know? And you ... were great."

Sarah leaned in to hug him, but David chose the wrong side. They laughed.

"Well. Good to see you."

"You too, Sarah. Thanks for stopping."

She wore a pretty summer dress. He watched her walk away. She was a knockout.

David retrieved the book once she was out of sight. Sometimes you didn't need a mirror to see yourself clearly.

Matty aced his English exam in spite of everything, He even achieved the highest mark in World History—Ancient Civilizations. His business class was a write-off. But he passed. And music was a no-brainer. It was his favourite.

This, he thought, would make his mother happy. But he couldn't really tell if she was happy or not. She'd been acting strange. Staring at him through meals. Telling him repeatedly that she was there if he needed to talk. One day, she even cleaned his room from top to bottom. He barely recognized the place.

He worried maybe she had found the pot, but it was still tucked in his socks when he checked.

The real test came over the Molson Park Festival.

Kim had managed to score four tickets to the Saturday show in Barrie. It was a reunion tour of sorts with bands like Pearl Jam, Soundgarden, and the Red Hot Chili Peppers.

He couldn't believe it. It took place at the end of July, a week before Matty was supposed to visit his dad.

He was dreading the visit. He couldn't even imagine two weeks without Kim.

And then his mother said no. And the visit to his dad's became the least of his worries.

"Why not?"

"It's hours from here and there's no adult supervision."

"Kim's an adult."

"Pardon me?"

"Well, she's eighteen."

"I don't care. She is not an adult."

Matty had even tried to work on Danny, who was traditionally a softer touch. But his mother got to him first. In the end, Matty did what he had to do. He packed a bag, stayed with Darius the night before the concert, and left early the next morning.

They grabbed Tina first, and then Kim.

Molson Park was a madhouse. Forty thousand people arriving by the busload.

The four of them were still stoned from the road. Darius and Matty and Tina took shifts. Kim didn't have a licence. For a while, she fell asleep on Matty's shoulder and he couldn't remember a time he'd been happier. The warmth of her head was like a second heart.

The first chords Matty heard struck a nerve and he could feel himself awakening. It was one of the opening acts. A local band. But already, the crowd was pulsing. The show started at four and ended at midnight with the Chili Peppers.

Kim looked positively elfin in the sun. Matty thought this must be what Woodstock felt like.

Darius shouted, "What are we waiting for? Let's go."

Inside the park things were even crazier. People were crowd surfing and the music hadn't even begun. There were several secondary stages set up around the edge of the park. One was a freak show where two guys took turns driving nails into each other's body parts.

"What the fuck," said Darius.

But they couldn't look away.

For a moment, there in the crowd and insanity, Matty thought about his mom. An hour from now she would be looking for him. Wondering why he hadn't called. Someone passed Kim a beer.

"Who was that?" asked Matty.

"I don't know."

Darius and Tina laughed.

Kim tipped it back like she'd done the first night Matty met her.

The crowd closest to them began a chant.

"Chug, chug, chug."

Kim gasped when she was through and then shook her head. A few people close by clapped and cheered.

"Woohoo!" she yelled. She wore cut-off jeans and a thin gauzy blouse. The black bra underneath was like a beacon.

Once the bands began for real, it became almost impossible to move. The four of them held hands and forced their way closer to the main stage near the end of the second local band. Some hairy guy passed Matty a joint and he took a drag.

He knew right away it wasn't pot, and passed it to Darius.

"Hash," his friend yelled and then smiled.

When Pearl Jam opened with "Alive" it was as though the crowd moved as one. During the solo in "Evenflow," Vedder leapt into the crowd. By the time he was presented back on stage, he had lost his shirt.

It was halfway through the set, when things slowed and the band played "Yellow Ledbetter," that Matty realized Kim was missing.

Darius shrugged. Tina shook her head.

"Don't worry about it, mother. She's a big girl."

But Matty couldn't let it go. When Pearl Jam left, so did he. He checked the merch tents and the concessions. He wandered over to the port-a-potties and hung out like a pervert.

He pedalled back toward the freak shows, but they were gone.

Along the way, he met a kid his age with long blond hair sitting cross-legged and alone under a tree.

"You okay?" Matty asked.

The kid could barely focus. He held up a piece of torn flannel. "It's Vedder's, man. Fuckin Eddie Vedder's shirt."

Matty moved on.

Although he heard the entire set, Matty didn't catch much of the Soundgarden show. He finally gave up and cut back into the crowd. It was dark now and the roadies were testing equipment for the Chili Peppers.

He'd almost given up on finding Darius and Tina when someone punched him in the shoulder.

"Man, where were you?" It was Darius.

Matty tried to relax and enjoy the show. He loved the Chili Peppers. Especially guitarist John Frusciante, who had returned to the band for their last album.

The heat was stifling. Darius had more hash. It went in and out of Matty's hands. After a while, he lost track of the individual songs. The area in front of the stage became a mosh pit. People slammed into him. He slammed back. Tina was lifted from the ground by a tall guy in a John Deere ball cap and beard. She floated around above them on a sea of hands. He had never been so thirsty. Eventually, he grabbed a plastic beer cup from a university-aged girl in the crowd, and quaffed it back. She had blond dreadlocks and a gap between her teeth. Her eyes rolled around in her head. He thought she might hit him when she raised her arm, but she offered him the peace sign instead.

Just before midnight, on their second encore, Anthony Kiedis asked the crowd to sit. And they did. Forty thousand fans sat down in the trampled grass, Indian-style. Steam was rising off the crowd. The band was down to their underwear, except for Frusciante, who wore denim coveralls and perhaps no underwear. Flea had broken a string on his bass and paced the stage with his arms crossed. It looked as though he was wearing an adult diaper.

Then, they played "Under The Bridge."

People held up lighters and cellphones. They swayed to and fro. The peace-sign girl sitting next to Matty put her arm around him and he did the same to her. Everyone was joining hands, hugging. Frusciante and the band launched into a prolonged instrumental interlude that was pure improvisation. It went on and on. The guitarist's fingers were otherworldly. Then Kiedis rejoined them and the crowd began to sing along.

The howl reached a crescendo as the last notes faded away.

"Fuck," said Darius, when it was over.

"Yeah," said Matty.

The entire crowd was numbed by it. They left in a daze.

Back at the pickup, the three of them waited and waited. The lot was emptying. Buses were loaded and pulling out. They climbed in the bed of the truck to wait and Tina leaned against Matty and drifted off.

And then, half an hour later, Kim came racing up behind them. She was wild-eyed and spastic.

"What's up?"

"I'm just coming down off a bad trip."

"What?"

"I met some guys. One of them gave me an acid tab."

"And you took it?"

Kim kept looking over her shoulder.

"She's fucked," said Tina.

Matty held her head the whole way home and stroked her hair until she fell asleep.

Danny was in Newfoundland for the weekend and Anne was going out of her mind. She called Darius around seven, but reached his father instead.

"Well, no. They're in Barrie at the Music Festival."

He probably thought Anne was a creature with nine heads.

"With Tina and that Kim girl. She's a wild one, that one."

Anne prepared herself an IsaLean shake. She craved its bubbly nothingness.

How could he do this to her?

And why was it that Darius Katsoulis's dad knew more about Kim than she did?

Anne had only met her once, and it was by chance. She'd come home early to prepare for an in-home consult with a potential customer and found them in the kitchen.

She thought immediately about what Camilla had said and then, after getting a good look at the girl, she thought, Oh god, Matty doesn't stand a chance.

Anne raised the shake to her lips and began counting the number of times she swallowed. Immediately she pitched the glass across the room, where it shattered against the base of the refrigerator.

She thought about calling David. She would be turning Matty over to him next week. But hearing his voice would only make it worse.

The refrigerator dripped sticky fluid on the floor. Anne walked toward it and pulled open the door. A pizza box sat on the bottom shelf. It must have been Matty's. She yanked it out from under the margarine and the jar of mayonnaise. The jar clattered but did not break.

Anne opened the box and grabbed a slice. Meat Lovers. Fuck it.

She bit into the pizza and her head hummed with endorphins.

She grabbed the last slice before she was finished chewing the first.

Then she went looking for a bag of chips. If she had any luck at all, they'd be all-dressed.

Matty approached his mother cautiously midway through the week. The last few days had not transpired exactly as he had envisioned them. Danny had come home on Monday, and the tirade Matty faced on Sunday replayed itself for his stepfather's benefit.

Danny had been angrier than Matty anticipated, but he suspected that Danny's anger was rooted in the fact that Matty had upset his mother and not so much by his attendance at the concert.

This led to a whole new level of conflict.

"You're never here!" his mother shouted.

"You knew what you were getting into. You know I don't have a choice. I have constituents to look after."

"Even when you're here, you're not here."

Tuesday, Kim would not return his calls or his text messages. And then on Wednesday, she did.

"*Maman*." He had not used French to address her since grade school.

She looked up from her tablet.

Kids were running through a sprinkler in the neighbours' yard. The screeching carried through the open window.

"Where's Danny?"

"He's staying in Ottawa. Is something wrong?"

Matty pulled out a chair and sat down opposite his mother.

"I know you're sorry."

"No."

"What?"

"I mean, yes. I'm sorry. But no, that's not why I'm here."

She made a noise in her throat.

"*Maman?*"

"Never mind. Go on."

Matty put his elbows on the table and used his hands to support his head. He was lost. Completely untethered. "Kim is pregnant."

When Matty looked back up, his mother was rubbing her eye.

"Did you hear me?"

"What do you mean, she's pregnant?" His mom was smiling. But not in any way happy.

"Well. She missed her period last week."

The inner workings were not yet solidified in Matty's head. "So yesterday she did a test."

"Is it yours?"

"*Maman!*"

"Don't *maman* me!" Her voice bordered on hysteria. "How did this happen?"

Matty cocked his head and rolled up his eyes.

Anne reached across the table. Her quickness surprised Matty and he jumped back.

"How did this happen?"

Matty could feel tears welling up in his eyes. His mother was already crying. She buried her head in her hands.

"But you had condoms."

"What?"

She lifted her head. Her cheeks were red and puffy. "I found one in the wash. Didn't you use them?"

Matty's mind raced. He looked away, considering.

"Well?"

"We borrowed some from Chloe once, and Darius. But, I was too embarrassed to buy them for myself. I never—I mean, I don't think ever…"

Anne allowed her arms to drop to her sides. Matty watched her muscles collapse. "Oh my god."

He did not understand what was happening. "*Maman*?"

"That fucker."

David flipped the pages of *Cosmo*. He'd finished his book on Sunday and the latest edition of *Model Railroader* wouldn't be in until next week. He stopped at "*Cosmo*'s Cleavage Wars." It looked promising. The subtitle posed the question, "Who rocked the hottest rack?" Enquiring minds wanted to know. Including David's. The article was short on text, but made up for it in glossy photographs of all the best cleavage shots to grace the magazine's cover. David was partial to Scarlett Johansson.

Then the telephone rang.

"Vermaelen's Dairy."

Salma Hayek wasn't anything to scoff at, either.

"We need to talk."

Hearing his wife's voice dropped into the store like a pebble irritated David. In all the years he'd worked there, he did not remember her ever calling him at work. She did not often call him at home. But once he was over his initial confusion, it occurred to him that something must be wrong. Monica Bellucci would have to wait.

"Is Matty all right?" The comforting hum of the compressor began to resemble the sound of rushing water.

"Define 'all right.'" Anne's voice had an edge to it. Anger. Not grief.

The water receded. He was expecting his son at the end of the week. "What did he do this time?"

Matty's recent dalliances did not register with David as they did with Anne. He had a hard time imagining them as part of his life. When Anne did choose to share information regarding Matty's schooling, or his lapses at school, David received them like news reports of distant events—striking civil servants in France, flooding in Bangladesh. Things that occurred, but bore no impact upon David.

"He got his girlfriend pregnant." The way Anne delivered the news made it sound as though the fault of this development lay with David. She continued to speak afterward, but he could not hear her over the rising water. "And, no, she isn't having an abortion."

The bell sounded above the door, and David lifted his head. An elderly man in a flat cap shuffled in.

"Are you listening to me? She's not having an abortion, because 'this baby's a gift.' Can you believe this girl? Her parents sure don't think it's gift. She showed up here last night with a suitcase."

"There's someone in the store."

"What?"

David glanced at the time on the register. It was 5:55 pm. Five minutes from closing.

"David. You can't run from this. He needs you."

"I know." David suddenly felt seasick.

"Your son is having a baby."

He hung up the phone without saying goodbye. Something in him switched to autopilot.

He tossed the magazine below the counter and turned around to fetch the keys to the front door. He could tell the man was just behind him, but he couldn't turn around.

"Could I get a King Size Player's Filter? While you're back there?"

David reached up. "Package or carton?" His voice seemed far away.

"Package. I'm trying to quit."

The old man laughed, until it turned into a cough. "Oh. And give me a pack of Life Savers, if ya got 'em. Peppermint."

David withdrew his hand and slowly turned around. The room, which had been spinning away from him, came into sharp focus.

The recognition was immediate and, David could tell, mutual. He stared directly into the milky blue eyes that would one day be his own.

Of course, it was his father.

The Road to Atlantis

David sat at the tiny kitchen table staring at a grimy tear in the linoleum. His father sat across from him. Between them was a bottle of Grant's Irish whisky. Six cans of Guinness were in the refrigerator. The table was a red pattern of Formica. The padded chairs did not match. The kitchen had not been redone since the 1950s, and the cupboards were thick with half a dozen coats of paint.

It had been three days since his father walked into the store. The man looked largely as David remembered him. Only older. He was bald from the forehead back now, and his hair was mostly white. He was slight with long frog-like fingers. His eyes were the same blue as David's, only further shot through with red and slightly cloudy at the edges.

He crossed his legs like a woman and his shoes had been purchased at Giant Tiger.

The man sucked his teeth. Most of them were still real. A few were missing in the upper denture.

For two people who had not spoken in thirty-one years, they had surprisingly little to say.

David had not stopped going to work each day, nor had his father stopped going to the Legion, where he drank two-dollar beer and played the occasional round of darts.

The only difference was that they both came back to the house on Water Street. And David's son was going to be a father.

"They say it might rain tomorrow."

David nodded. "Could be a thunderstorm."

The weather was his father's favourite topic. It was like a nervous tic. He did not seem comfortable with silence.

They had a lot of conversations about the weather.

David looked at the clock.

"They're late," Larry said. He fiddled with a pack of matches from the Village Idiot.

His father lived above a tavern in a single room with a shared bath. They went there together two nights ago after David closed the Dairy.

"That's Anne for you," David replied.

Half a dozen patrons stood smoking outside the front door. Larry wanted to join them for a quick one. "Can't smoke upstairs," he offered by way of explanation. He'd already smoked one on the walk over. He was a serial smoker. His mother had been as well. Cancer fixed that.

"Is she married?"

David shifted in his chair. "No. She lives with someone."

His room was on the third floor and there were no elevators. Larry stopped at the top of the first flight to catch his breath. "Keeps me young." He lifted his eyebrows and exhaled. "One more."

Before Larry found the key to let them in, David had already decided his father would not return to this place. The hallways smelt like urine. The carpet was worn through to plywood.

The room itself was neat and tidy. But it was stifling. The window, his father explained, was bolted in such a way as to allow no more than a crack of air. "Discourages the smokers."

He had a bed that dipped in the middle. On the other side of the room were a waist-height chest of drawers and a chair. A beer stein sat on the dresser. It was filled with pens. Beside it, a series of cheap watches were neatly placed in a row.

Everything the man owned fit into two garbage bags. David called a cab.

"I always thought your mother would outlive me."

David lifted his head, but his father's eyes were on the pack of matches. They were dangerously close to a real conversation. Outside, a car slowed to a stop. The tires rubbed against the curb.

David stood.

"Should I make myself scarce?"

"No."

Larry sat back and tried to disappear anyway. David thought he was good at it.

The car doors slammed in quick succession. He heard the pout of Matty's voice but not the words.

A moment later, there were footsteps on the porch. It was Anne. She still walked on her heels.

David strode past the living room to answer the front door, but his wife let herself in. David was not prepared for this. He hadn't seen her in years, except through the windshield of a car.

He stopped in the vestibule. She was very close. Dressed in a power suit—knee-length skirt and jacket.

Her head swung back and forth. Into the living room. Up the narrow staircase. "I think this is the first time I've come in."

She had slimmed down, and her face was angular and far more severe than David remembered. She'd dyed her hair a deep auburn brown with streaks of gold.

Both of her hands were wrapped around the strap of her purse, which hung from her shoulder.

"You look good."

"Well, I don't feel good." Her eyes came to rest on the baseball bat next to the door. "What's this?"

"Neighbourhood watch."

"Is that really necessary?"

David noticed a tic in her left eye.

"How's Danny?"

Anne looked out the open door to the car. "He's fucking his legislative assistant."

"Oh."

"Yeah. I guess it's going around."

David did not know what to do with his hands. He felt like a child in Anne's presence. He finally put them in his pockets.

"I'm moving out."

"Oh?"

"You already said that." Anne turned back to David. She looked him in the eyes. "It's going to be more than two weeks. I'm not asking. I'm telling you. You need to take him, David."

He could see a slice of the street past Anne, where a guitar lay propped against an army surplus duffle bag.

Then it occurred to David that he had heard three doors slam.

"Are you listening to me? I'm at the end of my rope."

The girl in the doorway was a tank top with legs. Nice legs. She barely had enough hair to pull into a ponytail. Her brown shoulders lifted into a shrug. When they did, David could see her tummy.

"So where do we put our things?" Two bags swung like pendulums at the end of her arms.

"We?"

The girl looked at Anne for help. Anne looked at David.

"My dad went ballistic. It's not safe for me there." She dropped the bags and stepped into the hallway with her hand out.

"Kim."

David wondered if he was the only person to think she looked like Angelina Jolie.

Matty appeared in the vestibule, sweating under a load of bags and suitcases. He dragged an amplifier over the threshold and dropped it on the floor.

He blinked, allowing his eyes to adjust to the darkness. "Who's that?"

Everyone looked past David.

Without turning, he spoke to Matty. "Say hello to your grandfather."

Then he pressed his fingers to the bridge of his nose.

Anne smiled at the women assembled before her. She may have even shown them crazy eyes. It gave people the false impression of impending euphoria. They were seated in a well-appointed living room. It whispered money, even if everything was a little too soft and floral for Anne's liking.

"So, ladies, what do you think?"

The entire Isagenix line was spread out on the coffee table before them—The 30-day Cleansing & Fat Burning System, Ionix Supreme. The whole shebang.

"These Whey Thins are amazing."

"Aren't they?" Whey Thins made Anne want to vomit.

"Me, it's the IsaLean Bars."

"Gotta cut those cravings, right?" She may have been overdoing the crazy eyes.

Meredith, the Whey Thin advocate, was already on board. Anne had met her at the gym. The others were all potential clients targeted by Meredith.

This crowd was interchangeable with the last. Women.

Middle-aged women. Not fat. Not lean. But battling against age. Weight. Fading beauty. They probably all had a stack of self-help books at their bedsides. The only one Anne could not peg down was a quiet woman who'd been introduced as Melanie. Maybe it was her lack of enthusiasm. Or the way she passed on the samples.

Anne viewed Isagenix parties like New Age Tupperware gatherings. Only of late she was beginning to feel a bit Machiavellian. Preying on these women's desire to lose weight. Feasting on their insecurities.

"But what about these wrinkles? A friend told me Isagenix could help with aging."

"Didn't I mention Product B?" Anne knew she hadn't. This was part of the performance. But wait ... there's more. Buy now and get a free set of steak knives.

"Have you ever heard of Telemere Support?"

"Is that how you keep your skin looking so young? Doesn't she have beautiful skin?"

Anne blushed dutifully.

"Gorgeous."

"Mmmm."

"You want Renewing Night Cream. It's my little secret."

"How much does this all cost?"

This was the lob ball Anne was looking for. This was where she hit one out of the park.

She could hear Camilla whispering in her ear, "This is where your bread's buttered."

Wealth creation. The products were ancillary to the scheme. A simple vehicle for the multi-layer marketing.

Suddenly, Anne didn't feel so well. They were hooked. All she had to do was reel them in.

"Could I get some water?"

Meredith stood and left for the kitchen.

"Anyone else find it hot in here?"

Karen was packing away her Whey Thin samples.

"Careful, dear. Why don't we share those around?"

Anne could feel the room titling away from her. Karen withdrew her hand from the bag and reluctantly passed them along.

Her life had become stranger than fiction. The pregnancy. Danny's infidelity. Seeing the shambles David had become. And the sudden reappearance of the heretofore unknown father-in-law. She didn't know whether to laugh or cry.

"Thank you, Meredith. You're a dear," Anne responded as she received her water. She began to count the number of times she swallowed.

Anne slammed the glass on the coffee table. All the women stared at her.

"Let's talk about the Business Builder Pack, shall we?"

By the end of the evening, Anne had moved a mountain of product. And aside from Meredith, she had three new recruits. Camilla would be proud.

The only dud turned out to be Melanie.

The women all spoke animatedly in the foyer of Meredith's home as they retrieved their bags and put on their shoes. They were still calling to each other as they made their way to their cars. Excited at the prospect of money and beauty.

As they drove off in their minivans, Anne finally exhaled. She laid both hands on her steering wheel and pressed her back into the plush leather seat. Then, she shook the vehicle violently, and screamed.

It was the delicate tap at her window that brought her back like a slap. Her hair was wild and tangled. A strand was stuck in her teeth. Without looking left, she slowly lowered the window and then turned with a smile.

It was Melanie.

Her eye whispered, *We're going to get through this.*

"I'm sorry. I just had to meet you."

Like the other women, Melanie was in her late forties. She had short, stylish hair, a pageboy cut. Her cheeks were fleshy, and so were her hands, which both lay on the edge of Anne's car door. The rings on her fingers sank deep.

"Pardon me?"

"You're Matty's mom, aren't you?"

Anne's mind spun like a Rolodex but could not come up with a match. "Yes. Do we know each other?"

"Kim is my daughter. I'm her mother. I am Kim's mother."

The news sank in.

"Do you drink red wine?"

Melanie nodded.

"Follow me. I've bottles of it at home."

Melanie was a bigger mess than Anne. Anne hardly thought it possible. At first, they sat in awkward silence, sipping Cabernet Franc from the Niagara Peninsula. But once she began, Melanie could not be stopped. Her voice had a breathless quality, as though she feared someone might overhear them. More than once she leaned in to share a particularly shocking piece of the story. And her hands did not stop moving. To fix her hair, which did not need fixing. To straighten her blouse, which did not need straightening. Even folded in her lap, they burrowed into each other like rodents.

In between chapters, Melanie would reach for the wineglass and drink in swallows. Anne looked away in case she began to count.

Kim was the reason they returned to Canada from Germany. "She was just so impulsive."

At seventeen, she was reading Goethe and Hesse and Scho-penhauer and hanging out at poetry readings with university students. Melanie wasn't even sure how they met.

Her philosophy teacher was a German national. He was thirty years old and married with two kids.

Kim ran away to Hungary with him. The police traced them through the man's credit card receipts. But eventually, it was Kim who called them from a village on Lake Balaton. He'd left her there with a few hundred euros. Got cold feet. Or missed his children. Melanie wasn't sure.

The expat community in Lahr is small. Everyone knew. Everyone watched the drama play itself out.

"Of course, we blame the teacher," assured Melanie. "He should have known better." She gulped her wine like a fish, the glass supported in both hands.

Anne counted out loud in her head.

Larry once sat in the cockpit of an SR-71 Blackbird stealth fighter. It was stationed on the tarmac of Uplands Airport in Ottawa. His employer, MEL Defence Systems, later to be purchased by Lockheed Martin, had brought the plane in as a publicity stunt. He and several colleagues from the contracts department drove out from Stittsville with civilian clients from the Department of National Defence. It looked like something right out of *Star Wars*. He remembered wishing Davy were with him as the American Air Force pilot strapped him into the seat. This was the closest he had ever come to joining the military, let alone a combat mission. And yet, decades later, he found himself in the comfort of Branch No. 560 of the Canadian Legion, sipping subsidized draught and shooting the shit with veterans twenty years older than him.

Bud Walsh had been the one to sponsor him initially. A veteran of the Korean War. He'd lived above the tavern in the room next to his. But now Bud was gone, and Larry was living with his son over on Water Street. Life just had a way of happening whether you wanted it or not. Larry had to shake his head in disbelief.

"What do you mean, no?"

Larry stared across the table at Scott Boileau. He'd lost the thread of whatever conversation the man was having. Gerry and Ken chuckled. Scott was still an active member of the forces, and the only person in the room younger than Larry. He'd fought in the Persian Gulf as a seaman on the HMS *Terra Nova*.

"Sorry?"

"Jesus. Why do I even bother?"

Back in 1991, Larry had drawn up the contracts to retrofit the HMS *Terra Nova* with a modern missile tracking system. He remembered the guys at Lockheed laughing at the destroyer's specs. Built during the Second World War, it weighed less than the deck gun of the USS *Wisconsin*.

"Well, it's been swell, gents." Ken pushed back his chair and rose slowly. He winced with the effort. Rheumatoid arthritis. "But the wife'll have an all-points bulletin out if I'm not back by supper."

Gerry nodded and placed one hand on the table. "Yup. Time to throw in the towel."

Both men had served with the Royal Canadian Artillery, as had Larry's father, as best he knew. Though he had never mentioned this to either man. They fought in the Scheldt. They were real vets.

Scott sat back in his chair. "You boys are a riot. What about you, Lare? Time for another? Game of darts, maybe?"

"Ahh..." On any other day, at any other time, Larry was always good for another. But ever since he moved in with Davy ... well, he wasn't exactly sure what the difference was.

"I know you don't have a wife waiting, so don't bother." Scott was a short man, but powerful. His forearms were bigger than Larry's biceps. "On me, for chrissakes."

Gerry and Ken waved from the doorway to the cloakroom.

"Actually, it's my son. He'll be waiting."

Scott looked at Larry. Hard. "You have a son? Around here?"

Larry nursed the last of his beer. It was flat and warm and lay on his tongue like a dead fish.

Scott sat up and raised his hands. "Hey. You don't wanna talk. We don't gotta talk."

This was part of what Larry enjoyed about spending his time with vets. Everyone was a good listener, but no one had to talk.

"And a grandson. Apparently."

"Oh?"

"Davy," Larry paused. "David would be about your age, I guess. Matty's still in high school."

"Yeah?"

Larry stumbled through a plausible version of events. He might even have believed it, on the whole. He didn't know what he believed anymore. Somewhere along the way, Scott purchased them two more beers.

"Shit. I haven't seen my dad in two years. Took a swing at me the last time. Can't even think why." Scott snorted a kind of half-laugh. "Drinking, I guess."

Larry played with the coaster on the table. He really needed a cigarette. He thought telling Scott might clarify things for him, but now he was only more confused. Seeing Davy for the first time felt like a sucker punch. It was as though he was a thief caught with his hand in the till, and all he'd wanted in the last few days was to assuage the guilt he felt for his behaviour. Now, it suddenly occurred to him that perhaps he was more than Davy could handle at the moment. That maybe he and Matty would be better off if Larry took the proverbial powder. Again. After all, the two of them had made it this far without his help.

"Listen," Scott said. "We can play darts next week."

"Huh?"

"You ought to go back to your son's place."

Larry looked at the floor. "Yeah? You think so?" He could tell that Scott was staring at him again.

"I know it's what I'd want. If I were David."

It was as though the young man had just read his mind.

Matty stumbled out of the bathroom and required both hands to steady himself. He could hear the hiss of the toilet as the tank refilled. The lights in the hall were poor and they hummed.

The stairs loomed. He had started drinking with his grandfather shortly before supper and never stopped. The whisky burned at first. He couldn't understand why anyone would drink it. But after a while, he began to appreciate it. Kim tried to make them all bacon and eggs for supper, but she burnt the bacon and set off the fire alarm. When David arrived, he opened all the windows. But even now the smell of burnt fat permeated the house.

Kim went to her room early in a pout, and David disappeared into the basement, leaving twenty dollars on the table for pizza.

Larry proposed a game of cards, and after some searching, they found some in a kitchen drawer. The deck was old and dog-eared, but it was complete. Matty could not picture his father playing cards and assumed that they came with the house—left over a decade ago when the previous tenant cleared out.

Matty turned right at the bottom of the stairs, because he had no choice. The ancient radiator slept at the foot beside the front door. Warm air drifted in through the screen. Cicadas sang in the glow of the streetlamp.

Matty's room was at the front of the little house. The radiance often kept him up at night. Lately, he had difficulty sleeping anyway.

His grandfather sat with his back to the hallway. When he left the house in the afternoons, he wore a grey-checked flat cap. Without it now, his hair looked like a snow-white halo.

When Matty asked where he'd been all his life, the old man shrugged and said that he worked in Colorado for many years.

He did not sound offended or particularly apologetic.

Larry's hands shook when they were idle, but not when he dealt cards.

They began with blackjack. Matty was familiar with it. Later, Larry showed him how to play gin rummy, spit, and two-player pinochle.

The man was a repository of dirty jokes. Some were so terribly racist they made Matty feel guilty for laughing. But others were simply funny. Larry knew how to tell a joke as well as he could play cards.

Every five minutes he stood and went out to the front porch for a cigarette. He moved slowly, a concentrated effort to appear sober. Eyes fixed on some unseen spot on the horizon.

Matty took up his place at the table.

Larry cleared his throat. "How about a game of Norwegian whist?" He did not wait to begin shuffling the cards.

"What do you think he does down there?" Matty stared at the basement door.

The old man sucked his teeth and craned his head like a turtle. Matty noticed for the first time that his grandfather's cheeks were wet.

Larry sniffed. "I don't ask."

"Grandpa?"

The man's hands faltered and a three of diamonds landed upright in front of Matty. Larry didn't seem to notice. Two rounds later, he looked at the arrangement of cards—rectangles of eight cards face down and another set face up. But the numbers were uneven. He still held cards in his hand.

His head bobbed and his lips worked like a rabbit's.

"Are you all right?" Matty could see plainly that he was crying, now.

"Time for a smoke break."

He had tried twice to rise from the chair and failed. Matty

rose to help him. The weight of the old man on his arm was almost nothing. When he was upright, he paused and placed his hand purposefully on Matty's shoulder. They were the same height. He gave it a squeeze before fixing his gaze on the end of the hallway and the streetlamp beyond.

It was more than he'd received from his father in a very long time.

David closed the basement door with a soft click. The kitchen was quiet except for the small motor in the wall clock that clicked like a hummingbird's heart.

Then he heard the peeling of the refrigerator door from its seal. He spun. Kim bent before the pool of yellow light. She was in her underwear. Matching black lingerie. It could have been an ad for Victoria's Secret.

David stood quietly in the dark outside the borders of the refrigerator's beams.

Modesty was not her best quality. The morning before, she had met him in the upstairs hallway wearing only a towel.

She had a sly smile that made David nervous. It occurred in only one corner of her mouth and was accompanied by one raised eyebrow, which said, "I know what you're thinking."

She had a relaxed, sanguine way of moving pelvis first into a room, as though she were treading a catwalk. The only things she kept hidden were her intentions and a smoking habit.

David had caught her stealing cigarettes from his father's pack. Rather than put them back, Kim palmed them and placed a finger over her lips. Turning David into an accomplice.

She retrieved the milk from the refrigerator and drank directly from the carton. She had a small tattoo at the base of her spine. A Japanese symbol. Light and dark.

"There are glasses in the cupboard."

She started and dipped forward into a bow to stop the milk from spilling.

Facing him, she stumbled back two steps and caught herself on the open door with her free hand. The light of the refrigerator blinked like an eye.

"You've been drinking."

"I thought you were in bed."

"Do you really think that's a good idea?"

She offered him the sly smile. "How long have you been watching me?"

"This is my house." David did not want to be forced into defending himself. "You have to start thinking about the baby."

"So now you're dispensing parenting advice. Matty should be here for this. What was your daughter's name again?"

David's voice caught behind a lump in his throat.

Kim tipped the milk up a second time, and then wiped the back of the hand across her mouth. Her legs cut like scissors down the hallway. She took the carton with her. The refrigerator gaped.

The next morning, David drew some small satisfaction when he heard the girl throwing up in the toilet.

Larry crept down the hallway to the bathroom. He didn't sleep much at night. Age, as much as anything, was the reason. He drifted off in the middle of conversations sometimes, but when it really mattered, no dice. He did not bother with the light switch. Davy had to work the next morning. He didn't want to impose. But he was beginning to like it here. The activity comforted him. Even if underneath it all, he sensed an iceberg lurking.

He searched in his underpants for his penis. Stood there coaxing it to work. He hated that. Lying in bed the need seemed urgent. Now he couldn't purchase a piss. He glanced around the tiny room. Bras and panties were strung up over the tub on a makeshift clothesline.

But for a brief period during his time in Littleton, Colorado, Larry had lived alone since leaving Davy's mother. His late wife. He wasn't good with people. Not in an intimate sense. Women especially. So he felt it wasn't his place to give advice to Matty. He didn't even know where to begin. But, Jesus, that boy was in trouble. What he wanted to say was, "Cut and run." But then, that was his trick. And a magician should never reveal his tricks.

Larry felt the beginnings of a trickle. He tried to relax.

Besides, Matty was a better man than Larry had ever been. Larry didn't know much. But he did know that.

Matty would never leave Kim, in spite of all her flaws. Perhaps he would never leave her because of her flaws. There was something of the healer in Matty. This he took from his grandmother. He even looked like the woman. And because of this, Larry was sure that the boy would never leave his own child. That took a cold mechanical precision. You had to be scalpel sharp with a selective memory. You had to be able to shut doors and never again test their handles. This wasn't in Matty.

Larry scared himself. He knew that he was capable of anything. The alcohol helped, of course. But now he feared that this ability had rubbed off on Davy. Larry did not have to be good with people to notice the chasm that existed between father and son. Maybe that was hereditary, too.

The first few drops of urine splattered in the bowl. And then nothing.

He thought about the cellar and what Davy might be up to down there. He could ask, or even sneak down while his son was at work. But something told him not to. That he didn't have the right.

Part of him still believed the magnanimous myth he told himself. In leaving, he was rescuing Davy and his mother from the monster that he was. In him lurked the same icebergs that he suspected floating through his son's house. They were just waiting to rub up against a hull in the middle of the night. He didn't trust water, and he didn't want to tear holes in his family. But after years of lying to himself on this front, he was ready to look in the mirror. Leaving was nothing but a selfish act. Full of self-loathing, sure. But the only person he was rescuing through jettison was himself. He couldn't stand measuring his own failures against the goodness of the people around him.

Larry felt a sudden flood of relief. A stream of urine rushed forth. He sighed and aimed for the side of the bowl, so as not to make too much noise.

In this life, he had to be thankful for small mercies.

David awoke from a dream. For a moment, it was there before him, full blown and real, and then it dissolved like sifted sand, grain by grain. He was diving again. On a reef. The water was warm and there were fish everywhere. Colourful and exotic. He couldn't remember how he had arrived there, but he was entranced by them. They beckoned. Without thinking, he followed. But the water grew quickly cold and the fish scuttled away. And then he was alone. When he looked down, the reef was gone. In its place was the nothingness of a starless sky. Empty blackness as far as he could see. He panicked and found he couldn't breathe. But as he tried to surface, he became confused and directionless. Instead of swimming upward, he delved deeper. He thought he saw a string of Christmas lights in the distance and made for them. Instead, he found the ruins of a Ferris wheel. Carousel horses sitting on the ocean floor. And an elephant, six stories tall—now the real estate of fish. It was foreign and familiar at the same time. Then he saw the upturned boat with the inverted writing. The one from their vacation. Only this time it read "Atlantis."

He swung his legs over the edge of the bed. The clock flickered 2:15. In the next room, he could hear his son's desperate grunting. Kim's soothing response.

He searched the floor for his shirt. The night air was still and close through his open window. Crickets creaked in the back yard.

The noise of their lovemaking was more apparent in the upper hall.

David was cautious on the stairs, descending against the wall to minimize the cracking of the steps.

That's when he heard someone fiddling with the latch on the screen door. He was normally careful with locks. Always double-checking before bed. But the main door was now open. He could not remember the series of events earlier in the evening, and it wouldn't have mattered anyway. The house had become a freeway of activity at all hours. Anyone could have opened it after he'd gone to bed.

Still on edge from his dream, David moved quietly but quickly to the bottom of the stairs. The baseball bat rested against the radiator. His hand was almost upon it when the door popped open reverberating loudly in its frame.

David pounced. His father shuffled in, glanced at the bat.

"Going to beat some sense into that boy?"

He didn't flinch.

"What are you doing up?"

David lowered the weapon.

"Someone ought to turn a hose on those cats upstairs."

David smiled. "You want a drink?"

"I'll pour."

David took down two different tumblers. He didn't have a complete set of anything. One of them had a colour picture of Donald Duck. If they tried, they could ignore the sounds carrying from the cold air return above the living room.

"I was a terrible father."

The admission caught David off guard. He raised his hand, as though to say "water under the bridge."

"No, it needs to be said. When your mother was pregnant with you, we got into a fight and I threw the sofa across the room. With her on it. Your grandfather had to come over and sit on me. The man weighed three hundred pounds, if he weighed one.

"Once I bought a set of encyclopaedias from a salesman. Cost me five hundred dollars. We didn't have five hundred dollars. I let bills pile up. Your mom was an infant. She didn't know anything."

David could not follow the logic but he remembered the encyclopaedias. Their green bindings lined up along a shelf. Those encyclopaedias were his favourite thing.

"But I loved you. Even after I left, I never stopped loving you. And it was damned hard at first. But it got easier. But not really. If you know what I mean.

"I don't know what I did to deserve this." He waved his hand at the kitchen, the house.

Someone flushed the upstairs toilet.

"You are a better man than me."

"No. No, I'm not."

Although he had not spoken about Natalie in years, she was always close to David. She inhabited every room he entered. She followed at a distance on his way to work. Sometimes, she was sitting at the edge of his bed when he awoke in the morning. Waiting for him. Some days were better than others.

He allowed the story to spill from him like water seeking the lowest point.

"I know why you left. I can't even look at Matty without feeling ashamed."

His father slid his hand along the Formica table top until it touched David's.

They sat that way a long while. The sun was up before they went to bed.

In September, Matty went back to school. Anne came by and took Kim shopping. Her tummy was just beginning to bulge. But the girl's breasts were enormous.

"The same thing happened to my mom," she said, lifting them as though gauging the ripeness of produce. "Matty's not complaining."

Anne's eye pulsed. *We're going to get through this.* She was one week into a cleanse, and she was starving.

"Have you spoken to your mom lately?"

"On the phone. I have to catch her when my dad's not home. I think he's disowned me."

Kim held up a pair of knee-length boots. "What do you think of these?"

"I was thinking about something a little more, well, maternal actually?" Anne held up a billowy white blouse.

"I'm pregnant. Not celibate."

In the end, Anne purchased several pairs of maternity leggings and a top. It was a pretty floral print, but split beneath the bosom to make room for the baby belly. No doubt it was meant to be worn over a stretch tee, but Kim said, "No way. I'm not hiding my belly. If people don't want to see it, they don't have to look."

They ate lunch at a café off Princess Street. It had a courtyard, and they sat at a table in the sun. Anne ordered white wine but was taken aback when Kim did the same. The waiter didn't bat an eye. The girl was eighteen going on thirty, and Anne could not fault the server. But the thought of her drinking while pregnant irked her. Nonetheless, she bit her tongue. It was, after all, a single glass of wine.

Even when she tried, Anne was confounded by Kim. Clearly she was intelligent, perhaps dangerously so. And yet in a practical sense she was still a child. Anne suggested, for instance, that perhaps it was time to retire the tank tops. In response, Kim asked, "Have you even read Kierkegaard, Anne?" Anne admitted that she, in fact, had no idea to whom she was referring. "I want to live my life authentically," she continued. "To be true to myself and not bow to the norms and pressures society places on me." Anne wanted to ask her what that had to do with boobs and tank tops, but she thought better of it.

Later, Anne inquired about morning sickness. Kim laid down her fork. Without guile, she responded, "You mean that happens to everyone?"

At the end of the meal, she reached into her purse and took out a cigarette.

"What are you doing?" It was out before Anne could think about it.

Kim spoke with the fag hanging from the corner of her lips. "Relax, it's allowed on the patio."

Anne snatched it from the girl's mouth. "You can't smoke when you're pregnant."

"Did David put you up to this?"

"What?"

"Because, if you ask me, David has taken an unnatural interest in my activities."

"I don't know what you're talking about. But that's my grandchild you're carrying, and I'm not about to let you harm him with this."

Anne crushed the cigarette in her fist. The women at the next table stopped talking.

"You're a Freudian wet dream."

"Pardon me?"

"Hysteria. Displacement. Transference. It's pathetic."

Anne cleared her throat. She was keenly aware of the spectacle they were becoming.

"We'll talk about this later."

"Why? I'm not embarrassed. Your daughter drowns less than twenty yards away from you so you bubble wrap your son to compensate. And now you want to do the same to my baby. If I get my way, you'll never even get close it."

Anne's intent was not to hurt. She only wanted the girl to stop talking. And in that respect, the slap worked. She half expected Kim to stand up and walk out. But she didn't. She sat perfectly still and smoothed the tablecloth in front of her.

Anne cleared her throat and repositioned her knife and fork. "You read too much."

David came home to discover that his living room had been converted to a studio. An easel stood where the coffee table had been and a twisted painting of a young man's face glared out at him. The oily smell of paint permeated the air. It was, David had to admit, a very good painting.

The noise coming from the kitchen warned him of company. At the small table, Kim was speaking animatedly—her hands floated like butterflies or ash. There were two guests. David recognized the face of the young man as the one in his living room. He was pale with tidy dark hair and a thin moustache. In spite of the Indian summer, he wore a tweed sports jacket with patches at the elbows.

"David. Come meet my friends. This is Marc, with a 'c.' And this is Jules."

The woman was even paler, with long blond hair, severely parted in the middle. It fell over her shoulders, interrupted only by a stark bang that ran across her forehead, just above thin dark eyebrows.

"They've come all the way from Ottawa."

They were also drinking David's beer.

"Where's Matty?"

"He started work at The Burger Joint."

When, during a train meeting, David mentioned his new housemates to Lou, the man revealed to him that he ran a franchise of The Burger Joint downtown. David had no idea. Lou offered to take on Matty. He also shared the reason for his own living conditions. Lou's mother was suffering through the advanced stages of MS and could no longer manage on her own. Lou could not cater to the needs of his parish and his mother, so he bought into the franchise with Dirk as a silent partner. He understood unexpected burdens, he said. Then he laid his hands on David's shoulders, and looked him in the eyes.

"If you ever need anything. Even just a sympathetic ear."

David thought he had probably been a very good minister. He could sure as hell build model trains.

"Will your friends be joining us for supper?"

"For Kraft Dinner and wieners?" Kim lowered her head and giggled, squinting in the direction of her friends. "I don't think so. Marc is taking us out to Chez Baggio." Kim squeezed the young man's hand.

David stared at them. He didn't like Marc. His reaction was visceral and immediate. "So how do you know Kim?"

All three exchanged glances. The girls giggled some more. Marc blew air through his lips and reclined into his chair. He threw one arm over the back and crossed his legs. "We—went to school together. At Canterbury."

Students who attended Canterbury High School simply referred to it as Canterbury. People in the area knew immediately to where they were referring. It was a specialist school for the arts—visual, dramatic, musical, literary. It even had a dance programme.

"Interesting. What did you study?"

"Well, Jules is an actress. I'm a writer."

"Really. Anything I'd be familiar with?"

Marc's face went flat. Jules's eyes shot from person to person and eventually to the hands in her lap.

Kim chimed in. "Not yet. But one day. Soon. Marc has been accepted to a residency at the Taos Writers' Retreat in New Mexico."

"That's a shame."

This time, all three stared at David.

"I mean it's a shame that you're going away. You just got here."

"It's not until next March."

David walked to the refrigerator and pulled open the door. A single Guinness remained. He took it. "Is that your car outside?"

Marc smiled and leaned forward. "The Triumph?"

"Yeah."

"Yeah."

"Nice. What year is it?" David cracked open the can.

"1980. It's got a 1493cc with an inline four."

David whistled. He knew nothing about cars. "It's in mint condition, huh?"

Marc nodded and then rolled his eyes at Kim when he thought David was not looking.

"So how's an unpublished author afford a ride like that?"

Marc frowned. David took a sip from his beer.

"It was a gift."

"Mom and dad?"

"Yeah."

David walked back toward the front door and took another sip. "Well. Don't let me keep you kids."

Marc was the first to stand. "We'll wait for you in the car, okay?"

"Okay. I'll just grab my jacket," said Kim.

Marc withdrew an iPhone from his coat pocket and looked at the screen.

David leaned over his shoulder. "Nice phone."

Larry found it difficult to say no to Kim. The first time she asked him for a cigarette, he had suggested that she think about quitting. She, in turn, suggested that he do something anatomically impossible to himself. Now he was her official pipeline to tobacco. She would do well in prison, he thought.

She also seemed to know when his pension cheque came in.

"Can I borrow twenty bucks, Lare?"

"Borrow?"

"Let's not discuss semantics. Can I have twenty bucks or not?"

He was no better than Matty when it came to resisting her charms. But she wasn't all bad, either. He understood why Davy didn't like her. He wasn't blind. But she was still a kid, despite her age. She should have been in college or university somewhere enjoying her freshman year. Instead, she was haunting the house on Water Street, bored out of her skull. Pregnant with another kid's child.

He pulled twenty dollars from his billfold.

What she needed was her parents. Or some functional facsimile. Larry didn't qualify, clearly. Davy wasn't interested. And from the little he had witnessed, Anne was more likely to kill her than nurture her.

"Come on. Let's get a coffee. My treat," she said, tucking the bill into her jeans pocket.

"How about something stronger?"

"Are you trying to corrupt me?"

"You can order a milk, straight up. Make mine a White Russian."

"Grab your coat."

The day before Larry had awakened from a nap on the sofa to find her sketching him. She was brilliant. Unlike her paintings, which were non-representational for the most part—and according to Larry, a bit weird—the drawing was better than a black-and-white photo. He just wasn't sure about the quality of the subject matter.

Life had not been easy on Larry. Or perhaps it was Larry who had not been easy on life.

They cut their way down to King Street and stopped at the Tim Hortons there. When Kim ordered the coffee, the older woman behind the counter asked her if one of them was decaf.

Larry bit his lip.

"Of course I want a decaf. Can't you see that I'm pregnant?"

Larry buried his hands in his pockets and looked at the floor. At least she was making the right decision.

Only the moment they stepped out the door with their coffees, Kim passed her cup to Larry and lit up a cigarette. When she took back the coffee, it was the wrong one. Larry was sure that this was not an error.

"Let's go down to the marina," she said, dangling the smoke from her mouth.

Larry followed her across the parking lot at a safe distance.

Even this late in the season, there were yachts sluicing against their moorings in the harbour. An ancient blockhouse stood watch over them. Seagulls chattered and cried overhead.

Kim sat on the stone wall overlooking it all and tucked her feet up underneath her bum. "You ever been to Prague, Lare?"

He stood behind her, off to the left, sipping his decaf coffee.

"Lots of people rave about Paris. But I don't see it." Kim

flicked the unfinished cigarette into the harbour. "Now Prague, on the other hand … that's a city."

Larry watched the cigarette bobbing in the surf, bereft.

"Did you ever just want to run away from it all? Take one of those boats, for instance—" She broke off in mid-sentence.

Larry shuffled his feet and tried not to look in her direction.

"I didn't mean … I was just thinking out loud."

Regret. It was an emotion he didn't think she had.

"Sure," he mumbled.

Kim looked back out at the harbour and the island beyond. Then she pulled her coat a little closer and hugged herself. The steam from her coffee circled her head.

No, he thought. She wasn't all bad. But she was dangerous. She was a lot like him.

Matty's grandfather had fallen asleep on the living room sofa in front of the little television set. It received four channels, but one of them managed to pick up *Coronation Street*. The man was crazy about *Coronation Street*. Matty couldn't follow it. It was worse than a soap opera. And the girls weren't even good-looking.

Now some old movie about aliens was on. The guy from *Mr. Holland's Opus* was in it. Only he was young. Matty watched *Mr. Holland's Opus* in music class once. It was all right. But he had missed the beginning of the alien movie, so he wasn't interested.

His grandfather snored in the bath of blue light. Last Sunday they had watched *Butch Cassidy and the Sundance Kid* on the snowy television while Kim napped. Now that was a good movie.

It was almost midnight. His dad had already gone to bed. Matty had missed him, having just finished the late shift at work. Matty had already been up to the room he shared with Kim, but she was not there. It was two weekends in a row that

Marc and Jules had been down from Ottawa. Matty had missed them both times because of work.

He checked the refrigerator out of boredom. David had adopted a new habit of chilling only a few cans of beer at a time. The rest he kept under the sink behind the waste. Uninterested in what he found, Matty closed the refrigerator.

Across the room was the door to the basement. Matty looked over his shoulder to the hallway. The blue light flickered. He listened to the stillness of the house. Quietly, he moved over the sticky linoleum and tested the handle. It turned loosely in its hasp. He listened again to the floor above him. The only sound was the low music from the television.

David had never expressly forbidden his entry to the basement. He'd never mentioned the basement at all. It was this fact that made Matty most curious. He twisted the knob until it sprang from its latch. And then he slowly pulled it back. Cool damp air swept past him. He stared into the dank well.

The wall inside the door was open laths of wood. Rough and furry. When he located the switch, Matty flicked it up. A meagre glow illuminated the base of the steps. He took the first step. It gave way slightly, like the spring of a diving board. He took another. The treads were narrow and the risers were open. He imagined a hand grasping his ankle, and then banished the childish thought. But not entirely.

Halfway down the stairs, the wall changed from wood to rubble stone. It was moist to the touch. Cobwebs laced the ceiling trusses. To his right the room opened.

Matty stood completely still. Unable to move. The movie upstairs was almost inaudible. The only real sound was the buzz of the incandescent light bulb. He did not know what he had expected. This was not it.

Matty had never seen anything like it. He didn't know what to think. It was a railroad in the cellar of their home. It was completely out of proportion with the scale of the room. It was impossible to walk all the way around it. It was so real and vivid that it was not real. It was surreal. There were homes and streets and vehicles in the streets. There were people.

It must have taken years.

Matty approached it for a closer look. Afraid almost to breathe. A portion of it was obviously under construction. It was one of the stations, he guessed. Four arched rooflines built in basswood—almost finished, but not yet painted. He half expected to see a little crane at work, swinging basswood girders into place. It was incredible. The materials for the construction sat nearby in an alcove beneath the stairs.

And then he saw the train. Matty reached out as though he were not in control of his own limbs. He was compelled. Carefully, he lifted the engine from its track. The cars behind came with it. His heart jumped. He stopped and unhooked them. The machine was the length of his forearm. It had real weight. The paint had been dry-brushed to provide the illusion of dirt and rust. He scrutinized the rest of the diorama. Everything had been treated this way. The roadways had potholes, oil stains. The buildings bore the ravages of soot.

Matty replaced the engine and stepped back. His back pressed against the cool stone wall. His throat hurt. He clenched his teeth. For a moment, he closed his eyes and then drove both hands through his hair. They joined at the back of his head and he stayed this way. He was angry. Or maybe he was infinitely sad.

He was both at once.

Why had he never seen this before? How old had he been when it was started? His mind flung into every corner of the room. How many visits had he made to his father's over the years while this slowly grew into being under his feet? He would have loved this as a child. He loved it now.

They could have built this together. But they didn't. And they never would. Because he was seventeen and expecting a child of his own. Because that train had already left the station.

Because his father didn't care to ask.

Nat dressed in the most outrageous colours. Anne bought her outfits, matching tops and bottoms. Skirts with coordinated cardigans. Scarves and summer dresses. It didn't matter. She had her own sense of style.

Purple tights with pink dresses. Shorts and tiny cowboy boots. Stripes with polka dots or floral prints.

Nat raided her mother's closet too. Silk blouses became knee-length dresses cinched with studded leather belts. And because Anne sought order in all things, and Nat could not throw anything away, the house had a Halloween costume box as well—where she could seek feather boas and fairy wings.

Once a month Nat's school held "no uniform" days. These became battles. A test of wills. The evening before transformed into a fashion parade with edge.

"You can't wear those shoes with those pants," Anne said from the sofa.

"That green clashes with the blue in that shirt."

"Nat. Heels? Really?"

The final result was a hard-fought compromise. Both parties exhausted and a little shaken from the ordeal.

Anne could see herself echoed in her daughter. It was glorious and awful. A caged bird flexing unused wings.

Larry asked Matty to play something for him on the guitar. The boy was sitting on the sunken sofa in the living room. He didn't know where Kim was.

"It's not plugged in."

Larry sat in the armchair across the room. He was just back from the Legion, and a little drunk. "I'll be quiet."

Matty smiled. He was wearing a T-shirt with a print of Che Guevara, a pair of tattered jeans. "Got any requests?" The boy's hands flew over the fingerboard, snapping off a quick blues riff.

"You know any Willie Nelson?"

Matty let his picking hand fall to his lap and slung his head in Larry's direction. "You're kidding, right? Willie Nelson?"

"The man has perfect pitch." Larry was only a little hurt.

"The man's a country singer. I'm a rock star. There's no future in this relationship."

It was Larry's turn to smile. "So. No country, then?"

Matty licked his lips. "Wait." He went through the motions of tuning his guitar. Cocking his head in close to the strings. Then he ran through a quick progression of chords with his eyes closed, as if reminding himself of something. Larry thought he recognized it.

"Okay. It's not exactly country. But ... whatever. You probably know it. It's old."

They locked eyes and both smiled.

"Fair enough."

Matty took a breath. The song began with a low thrum and a hiccup, and then went into a funky slide. Larry was sure he knew it now. After a few repetitions of the opening bars, Matty began to sing in a voice that was thin and trembling, as though he were imitating the original.

It caused Larry to shiver. The guitar, which had no acoustic quality, was soft, but insistent. Matty could pick as well as strum. And he was throwing all kinds of little pull-offs and riffs in between the verses. Maybe he was showing off for Larry. Maybe not.

When he reached the chorus, Larry wasn't sure whether the boy's voice would crack. It teetered on some sort of sonic edge, and the lyrics made the hair on his arms stand on end.

Part of Larry wanted the boy to finish before Davy arrived. Another part of him didn't want the song to ever end. It filled the little room with its yearning.

And then Matty went into a prolonged solo, while balancing the rhythm with his thumb and a steady tapping of his foot. Larry wasn't sure if he'd heard the front door or not. But no one appeared in the hall. He was mesmerized by his grandson's talent. And just when he thought the song might indeed never end, the boy's hands slowed, and he sang again.

He held the last note impossibly long, and then it was over. And the house was still.

Larry didn't know what to say. It was a fragile performance, full of vulnerability. And it reminded him of everything he had missed out on over the years.

Matty shrugged and set the guitar against the sofa. "Anyway, it goes something like that."

Unmistakeably then, Larry heard the stairs in the front hallway creak. David was home and had been listening to his son play Neil Young's "Down By The River."

"That shit's messed up." Darius sat crossed-legged on Matty's bed.

Matty leaned on his guitar, contemplating the floor. "I know."

"And she's up there right now?"

"Yeah."

"At Marc's place?"

"No. She's staying with Jules."

"Or so she says."

"Fuck you."

Tina, who was lying next to Darius on the bed, punched him.

"Sorry, man."

Darius reached into his pocket for a package of cigarettes. He pulled out a perfectly rolled joint and raised his eyebrows. "Yes?"

"Fuck, no. What's with you? It's my dad's house, man."

Tina weighed in. "You're such an idiot sometimes."

"Glad I dropped by."

Matty stood and placed the guitar in its cradle. "She keeps saying that we gotta get outa here. That we have to go to Taos."

Tina scrunched up her face. "Where the hell is Taos?"

"New Mexico. I don't know."

Darius slapped Tina with a pillow, and a moment later they were rolling around on Matty's bed.

They might as well, thought Matty. He and Kim weren't doing much of that lately. It was December and she was really showing. Sometimes she asked Matty to place his head on her belly and listen for a kick. At other times, she was throwing shit at him. And not playfully. Last week, she kicked a hole in the speaker of his amp. It was now an ugly night table.

Sometimes he would lie awake just watching her. That seemed to be the safest bet.

When Marc and Jules didn't come down, she was angry and depressed. When they did make it, Matty never saw her. Two weeks earlier she came into his work on a Saturday night. He thought that she had probably been drinking, but he didn't want to confront her with it in a public place. She'd been really good about it lately anyway. Ever since his mother took her shopping for maternity clothes.

"We have to talk."

"Here? Can't it wait till I'm home?"

Marc entered behind her. And Matty felt that familiar sinking feeling he experienced every time he was around.

"Where's Jules?"

"What? Oh. I don't know. She didn't come down."

Marc did not wave or acknowledge Matty in any way. He took a seat in a window booth.

"What is it?"

"Marc's getting a place of his own."

"Yeah?"

"And he said we could come and stay with him."

"Stay where? In Ottawa?"

"Oh, my God, no. In New Mexico."

"Are you crazy? What about my school? And how are we going to make money?"

"He said you'd be like this."

"Who said? Marc said? Be like what? Sane?"

Marc was dressed in a dark blue pea coat with an elaborate scarf. He stared out the window and yawned.

A customer came through the door. And then another.

"You know that residency is bullshit, don't you? My dad looked it up. You pay to attend Taos. Anyone with a cheque gets in."

"Your work undergoes critical review before acceptance." Her long lashes were wet with melting snow.

"Look. Let's talk about it tonight. Okay?"

"I'll be out late. Don't wait up." She had a new way of walking, and he thought it was beautiful.

The Village Idiot was a pub, or a tavern, really. It didn't have the pretence of pub. David agreed to meet Lou there on Christmas Eve after he closed the Dairy. Vermaelen had given him an envelope earlier in the evening, as he had on every Christmas over the past few years. It was his bonus. It felt a little thicker this year. David put it down to Vermaelen's knowledge of the new circumstances in David's home. He hadn't counted it yet.

Lou had a table in the back. What used to be the smoking section, when smoking in taverns had been legal. It was carpeted in green and smooth as a pool table. The ceiling was low. The Idiot was walking distance to both men's homes. It was that simple. Neither held much affection for it. The bar was in the front. It had a darts league. A television played the hockey game. The back was quieter.

There were not many others this evening.

"Merry Christmas."

Lou stood at the sound of David's voice. "Merry Christmas, David. We've missed you at the club."

David removed his coat. "Sorry, I've—"

"Nonsense. Nothing to be sorry about. We all understand."

A woman in her fifties came to take David's order. She was wearing a Santa hat and leather pants.

"Grants. Thanks."

Music drifted back from the bar area—"Baby, It's Cold Outside." David always found the song a little creepy.

"My manager says Matty's doing a bang-up job, by the way. Can't say enough good about him."

"Thanks, Lou. For everything."

The man waved him off. "What are friends for, right?"

After two drinks and an in-depth discussion of Dirk's D & H Adirondack Operations Scheme, David excused himself in order to use the men's room. He re-entered the bar and descended the staircase to the basement. Another man followed him at a distance.

The facilities were tight at the Idiot. A urinal and a stall. David took the urinal. The smell of piss and sewage was only vaguely shrouded by chlorine pucks. Someone had hung mistletoe from the brass flush handle. Above the urinal was an ad for the Acura Infinity. They hadn't done their market research, thought David.

Only as he was finishing did David realize that no one was in the stall beside him. He glanced backward. A man leaned on the sink. He wore a beat-up ball cap.

David turned. "Merry Christmas."

"Remember me?"

David looked at the man's face. Good looking, but worn,

hollow cheeks. Two days' stubble. Dark eyes and hair. A gash for a mouth. High cheekbones. He wore a plain red T-shirt and jeans. Although he was thin, he looked tough as nails. Both of his forearms were tattooed in sleeves of red and green and black designs. David thought there was a naked woman in one of them. He was maybe thirty.

David cleared his throat. As well as a university, the town also had a couple of prisons. "Should I?"

The man rubbed his chin. He grinned and shook his head. "I'm disappointed in you, Mr. Henry."

It was Dallas Desaulniers. David's face changed.

"Wait a minute. I think it's coming back to you now. Am I right?"

David nodded.

"Small world, eh?"

The strains of "Run Run Rudolph" poured down the stairs. The tap behind Dallas was dripping.

"Listen. I saw you come in earlier, but I didn't want to interrupt. But seeing that it's Christmas and all, I thought maybe I'd give you something I've been holding onto for a while."

Dallas threw a better punch than David. Much better. He suspected practice. It was so quick that David was on his knees before he knew it had actually been thrown. The pain came afterward in a burst of white. He didn't know whether to shit or vomit. Mostly, he just worried about breathing, the other functions would surely take care of themselves.

The punch hit him square in the diaphragm. A second later he was folded over on the floor, his right cheek resting in a puddle of what he hoped was water from the sink.

Dallas stepped over him, and David listened as he pissed into the urinal. When the man turned to wash his hands, David had not moved. Dallas's boots were inches from his nose. Before leaving, he dried his hands on a paper towel and checked his teeth in the mirror. He stepped over David without so much as a word, and disappeared.

Larry intercepted him on the front steps. He had the last gasp of a cigarette in his hand. It was Christmas Eve and it was cold. But clear. It was only six thirty, but already it was black. Orion's belt flickered in the sky above the house.

"There's a note in the kitchen."

David felt the water rising, the sound of surf in his ears. His insides hurt.

"Where's Matty?"

"Not here. Not yet."

He left his father on the porch and entered the house. He supported himself with one hand on the wall as he struggled to remove his boots, cringing. The coloured lights blinked randomly on the little artificial tree in the living room. The presents appeared forlorn. They looked as though they had been wrapped by men.

The note was written on a leaf of paper torn from a pocketbook.

> Dear Matty,
>
> A relationship must have room for choice. I hope that you will respect mine. This baby has come between us and I don't think I want it to be raised in that kind of environment. I need room to think. I'm moving in with Jules for now. Her parents have been great. I don't know what I'll do after or where I'll go. But for now this just feels right.
>
> Kim

David shook his head. He reread the note. The girl was off her rocker. Then he heard the front door open.

"What's wrong?" It was Matty.

Larry was shuffling in not far behind.

"You better sit down."

"Where is she?"

Larry started coughing and couldn't stop.

"Are you all right?"

"Is she gone? She's gone, isn't she?"

"Matty, take off your coat."

"Why won't you answer me?" He looked at the paper in David's hand. "Is that from her?"

David held it up as though for the first time.

"Give it to me."

Larry pulled out a chair and sat. He was still trying to clear his throat.

Matty looked up. "What the fuck does that mean?"

"I don't know."

"What do you mean you don't know?"

David rubbed his face with his hand.

"That's what you've got for me?" Matty tossed the paper. Undramatically, it flipped and slipped under the table onto the floor. "Nothing."

He could not look at his son. Larry too, though calmer now, considered the pattern in the linoleum.

"Well, that's just great. I suppose I should expect as much." Matty grabbed the back of a chair and tossed it across the room. It smashed into the cupboards where David hid the beer.

"You know what Kim called you guys? Huh? Emotional dwarves. I didn't fuckin get it at the time. But now I do."

"Kim said a lot of things."

"What the fuck is that supposed to mean?"

Larry tried to grab Matty's sleeve. "Have a seat, son."

But Matty shook him off. "Don't fuckin touch me. You think you can show up, share a few beers and then act like it's all cool? You are fucked up. Go watch *Coronation Street*."

"Matty, that's enough."

"Oh, are you gonna be my dad now? Great fuckin time to start."

"Matty."

"Sorry. I'm not Natalie. I'll never be Natalie."

"What are you talking about?"

"You know why? Because she's fuckin dead. And we have no idea what she'd be like now. Try living up to that."

David watched something change in his son's face. It was a decision. He turned and stormed off in the direction of the front door.

"Matty," David called after him.

But he did not leave. He stooped and then came straight back to the kitchen. In his hand was the bat.

David took two steps backward, but Matty was moving quickly. He was past his father before he could react. The boy threw open the door to the cellar and stabbed at the light switch.

David followed him down the stairs. He could hear Larry not far behind.

If David had wanted to stop him, it would have been possible. Matty paused at the bottom of the stairs. He looked at David, and even after he lifted the bat, there was a moment of suspended animation. Then he set his teeth and swung.

The first blow caused the entire structure to jump. But not nearly as much as David expected. The railroad was heavy, and the ceiling was low. Matty could not gather enough momentum. The second swing landed at an angle and swept away the support beam for the Manchester Piccadilly Station. It collapsed, crushing shops and a portion of the track.

Matty moved further into the room. David entered behind

him, but stepped into the recess with the furnace as though to observe. Larry didn't know what to do, so he sat on the stairs, breathing heavily, mouth open.

Blow after blow rained down upon the tiny world David constructed. Bits of plastic and wood splintered. Matty sent the Coronation Scot flying into the wall with all its cars attached. The arched roof of the Piccadilly train sheds exploded in a rain of basswood sticks.

As the interval between swings lengthened, David could hear his son sobbing. He was exhausted, and barely able to catch his breath. His face was wet. Spittle on his chin and in the corners of his mouth. After a while, the bat was simply shuffling rubble from the corkboard to the floor. And then it came to rest. Matty released it, and it slid off the edge and out of sight against the wall.

In that moment, David thought about the beach all those years ago. And he thought about the little boy beside him. Tired and sunburnt in his bright orange water wings. Confused and curious. A victim. As much as David. As much as Anne. As much as the little girl lying awkwardly in the sand.

David then did what he should have done years ago. He took the boy into his arms. And together they cried.

Larry used to spend Saturdays out driving the concession roads with Davy. He piloted the little Dodge Dart with one hand. With the other he steadied a beer bottle between his legs. Davy was still quite young in those days—seven or eight. Impressionable. Scared. But happy. Part of the adventure involved speed and the feeling they could achieve as the Dart skipped over mounds in the pavement like a roller coaster. Part of it was the wind whipping in through the open windows. The arteries of wood-beam fences clipping past. Forest and open fields.

They often packed a lunch, or maybe his wife did it for them.

He remembered a yellow nylon backpack from McDonald's with red straps. Frequently they stopped at an old quarry north of town—an ill-used sand pit owned by Cavanaugh Construction. If time allowed, they would hike up the steep banks and into the brake along the edge. Beyond, there was pasture and a two-track road passing through a dale. Larry told his son that it was a trail used by moonshine runners, something the boy would understand from *The Dukes of Hazzard*.

One afternoon, when they came across the old red pickup of the farmer, bumping along the tracks, he had the boy crouch in the underbrush.

"Careful," he'd whispered. "We don't want them to see us."

And dutifully, Davy sat still as a stone. Larry could feel the boy's accelerated heartbeat through his shirt, hand on his back.

On other occasions, he let the boy drive the car in the base of the pit, propped up between his legs. Like this, the car would kick up dust as it spun and turned erratically in search of a path. If Davy came too close to a sapling or a mound of earth and rock, Larry could lay his hands over the boy's and guide them gently in the right direction.

When he was tall enough to reach the pedals on his own, Davy begged Larry for the opportunity drive the car all on his own. It was after their picnic, and in the wake of a fresh beer. Hoping to extend the good feeling they had established, Larry acquiesced. And for the first time, he watched Davy from the passenger seat. The furrowed brow and the intensity in his son's eyes confused him at first. The same elation, the squeals of joy, normally elicited by the whir of the tires on sand had disappeared. Instead, Davy sucked his lips, tension visible in the abrupt movements of his shoulders.

And then it happened. Davy tried to pull out of a doughnut but lost control of the wheel. Larry watched in a fog as his son swung the vehicle left and right in search of equilibrium. A second later, the front end was buried in a bank of sand. Silting like a shipwreck.

Davy sniffled in the seat beside him. "Why didn't you grab the wheel?"

The memory of that moment had grown in significance over the years, until it became a metaphor for everything that characterized Larry. Now, however, he could see it for what it truly was. He saw it as a father should. As a metaphor for everything that characterized his son, and what he had done to him.

Melanie would not return Anne's messages. Her texts went unanswered. Two weeks after Kim's disappearance Anne drove to their home, a foreboding Victorian brownstone on the corner of Lake Avenue. Two cars sat parked in the laneway. There were lights on in the first floor. The sidewalk to the back door was cleared of snow, so Anne chose to knock there first.

It led onto a large modern kitchen. In the middle was an island. Evidence of meal preparations. Pots. Oven mitts. A half bottle of cooking wine.

A dog barked down the street. Anne was about to knock a second time when a young adolescent materialized. She paused in the doorway and peered through the window at Anne. For a moment, the girl did nothing. Then she glanced backward over her shoulder into the room from where she had arrived. And then she was gone.

After what seemed like a long time, but was really less than a minute, Melanie appeared in her place. She did not look up until she reached the back door.

Anne could hear the lock click feckless. She opened the door enough to allow her head and shoulders through.

"Good evening, Anne. I'm afraid now isn't a good time."

"Just tell me. Is she here?"

"Kim?"

"Of course, Kim. Who else is there?"

"No."

"No? No she's not here?"

"Yes."

Anne's eye throbbed. She said each word slowly. "Is Kim living at home with you?"

"I don't think you understand. My husband—" Melanie stole a look backward to where her daughter had been earlier.

"You know that she left David's? That she's no longer with Matty?"

Melanie whispered, "She called me around Christmas."

"You know where she is?"

"She's in Ottawa. At a friend's. Please understand. She's asked me not to tell Matty. My husband doesn't know. He doesn't want to know. It's as though he no longer has a daughter." Melanie's voice broke, but she mastered herself.

Anne heard footsteps. Melanie took a step away and pushed the door into its frame. Before it could catch, Kim's father was there. The door opened to its full extent.

He was a man of medium height and slender build. He wore beige trousers and a checked shirt open at the neck. His hair was dark grey with silver highlights. Like Camilla, he had crazy eyes. And they darted up and down the street before lighting on Anne.

"We're in the middle of supper. If you continue to harass us I will call the police. Do not phone. Do not visit. I don't know what it is that you want from us, from my wife. But I'm sure we cannot help." The man took another look up and down the street before retreating and closing the door.

The younger sister was again in the kitchen, arms folded. Her father took her by the arm and led her back into the dining room. Melanie followed, glancing back only once at Anne, who had not moved.

On the way back across town, she pulled up to the curb in front of a convenience store and turned off the ignition. She was tired. And she was hungry. Parliament was back in session and she had been on autopilot all week. The IsaLean shake she had had for lunch was a distant memory.

Anne stepped over the snowbank and into the slush. An electronic bell sounded when she entered. In the back, behind glass doors, she found the McCain's cake she was looking for. Double Chocolate. In university she and David used to feast on them together. Eschewing plates, they each picked away with a fork, talking about life and the future, until it was gone.

Back in the car again she laid her purchase on the passenger seat and started the engine. She set her hands on the wheel but did not move. Outside the store stood a garbage can overflowing with refuse. She considered tossing the cake.

Instead, she killed the engine. The cake taunted her from within the plastic bag. Anne slid the box out and peeled back the foil edges. With one finger, she swiped the cool icing and stuck it in her mouth. She had been chewing her own teeth since morning, and the gratification was instant. She took another swipe. Then she sank all five fingers knuckle-deep into the moist heart of the dessert and tore it loose.

Seven days before Matty's birthday, David received a call. It was the Ottawa General Hospital. The small voice on the other end was hesitant.

"My name is Christine Gamble. I work with Child and Youth Services. Are you David Henry?"

It was the first week of March. Outside it was snowing heavily. The school buses had been cancelled and although Matty walked, he did not bother getting out of bed. It was now almost noon. David remembered the secret joy he had felt on mornings such as these when he was a teacher. The calm sense of communion he experienced sitting alone in his classroom, marking papers or preparing lessons.

Because it was Monday David, too, did not leave the house. In the other room Larry watched *Coronation Street.*

"Your name and number is all we have."

The familiar sound of the tide rose in David's ears. "My name?"

Kim had had the baby three weeks early. She had checked into the General on Friday. The contractions were slow, but she had begun to dilate. She was given a room.

"A friend was with her the entire time."

"Jules?"

"No. It was a young man."

David felt submerged. He could barely hear the woman on the other end over the roar of the surf.

"Could you just tell me, is the baby all right?"

"Oh, yes. Yes. I'm sorry. The baby is perfectly healthy. We have her here at the hospital.

"Her?"

"Yes, sir. It's a baby girl."

"And *you* have her?"

"Well. That's why I'm calling. Miss Sheffield—Kim—she left sometime during the night."

David let this last piece of information sink in. "Then how did you acquire my name and number?"

"It's on the admission papers as an emergency contact."

"I don't understand."

"Are you a relative?"

David paused. "Yes. Yes, I am. I'm the baby's grandfather."

The four men sat in the tiny Volkswagen as it idled at a light. David in the passenger seat. Larry and Matty, who looked washed out, in the back. Lou drove.

The road was empty. Snow arrived from all directions, blown in gusts. It was painfully quiet in the car. When the light finally turned, the little vehicle spun and spun, inching its way through the intersection. Lou gave it more gas, but that only caused the rear end to slide out. Ruts of unploughed slush stretched out before them.

"You sure about this?" David asked.

Lou glanced over once the tires took hold. "We'll get there."

He must have been a *really* good minister.

The highway was worse. Tractor trailers sped past. The car rocked. They were practically skating.

David watched Lou look up into the rear-view mirror. "I suppose congratulations are in order."

Matty blinked as though startled from a reverie. "Huh?"

"How does it feel to be a father?"

David took stock of the automobile's occupants. Lou was asking the wrong crowd.

It took them half an hour, or double the time to reach Gananoque. The windshield on Lou's little car was freezing up. Vehicles swirled in and out of view, beginning and ending as dots of lights in a blast of snow. The wipers clacked at the beginning and end of each cycle.

Lou turned on the radio to calm everyone's nerves, but the first station on the preset was a religious call-in programme. David stared at his friend.

Lou smiled and dialled in something else. The first strains of Willie Nelson filled the vehicle as it was rocked by a passing tractor-trailer.

Larry chimed in, "Now that's better."

"Oh, my god." Matty buried his head in his hands.

"Not a fan?" Lou asked.

"Watch out," David said, over the music. "The traffic is stopped ahead."

Just then, a dark pickup truck barrelled past in the adjacent lane, seemingly oblivious to the weather or the road conditions.

Lou sucked air through his teeth. "Oh, my."

A grey sedan followed close behind.

Matty looked up. The sedan broke hard and fishtailed in front of them. The sound of the pickup's impact was like a tray of dishes dropped on the floor.

"Watch it!" David grabbed the dash with both hands.

A second later Lou swerved to miss the slipping sedan, which was halfway across their lane. In the back, Larry groaned, and the screech of his son's scream sounded almost feminine.

David watched the world spin around the gyre of Lou's car. Trees. Another truck. A set of headlights. He thought he might be sick, so he closed his eyes.

Immediately after she hung up the phone with David, Anne decided that she would confront Melanie. She could hardly believe that her granddaughter was spending the first days of her life alone in a hospital full of strangers. And now Matty would be on the road in the worst snowstorm of the season.

She entered the kitchen and tapped each burner on the stovetop even though she could see plainly that they were off. In the hallway, she grabbed her phone from the table. There were five text messages from Danny. She erased them and fired off one of her own to Melanie.

"I'm coming over."

She locked the door of her apartment and shook the door to test it. Halfway to the car, she turned back to shake it one last time. As she pushed through the snowdrifts down her walkway, she suddenly became conscious of counting her steps.

"Goddamnit." She kicked at the snow repeatedly, until she felt better. Across the street, her elderly neighbour, Mrs. McIntosh, stood still, a snow shovel in one hand.

Anne smiled. "Good afternoon."

The woman slowly raised her hand.

"Fuck. Fuck. Fuck," she thought, as she began cleaning her car.

She was only three minutes away, but as Anne eased the vehicle onto Lake Avenue, Anne caught Melanie backing out of her laneway. Anne flashed her lights and honked. Melanie's car did not stop. A moment later, the two women were facing one another head on.

Anne waved frantically. And for a brief instant their eyes met. Melanie put the vehicle into drive.

"You little—" Without thinking, Anne veered into the other woman's lane. Her eye twitched, so Anne put her foot to the floor.

The resulting collision detonated the car's airbag. The noise was terrific. It was as though someone had just crushed a giant beer can.

When her head stopped buzzing, Anne watched Melanie struggling to free herself from her seat belt. She looked up at Anne, mouth wide in disbelief. And then she undertook her struggle with renewed vigour.

Anne's driver side door was stuck, so she climbed across the console and pushed open the passenger side. Melanie stumbled into the snow. Seeing Anne so near, the woman panicked and held up her purse as a shield. "You're crazy."

"Where is she?"

"What are you talking about?"

"Do you really think lying is the best course of action under these circumstances?" Anne looked at the smoking wreckage of the two cars and then back to Melanie. She lifted an eyebrow.

"She's with Marc. They've left for New Mexico. They're driving."

"Did she tell you that she left the baby behind?"

A car slowed in the adjacent street.

Melanie's voice sounded small and very far away. "Yes."

"And you think I'm crazy?" Anne reached into her coat pocket for her phone.

The car came to a stop and backed up. Slowly its window lowered. "Are you okay?"

Anne looked up. "Never better."

Melanie said something behind her, but Anne did not hear it over the car's engine. She turned. "What?"

"Is it a boy or a girl?"

"She didn't tell you?"

Melanie shook her head. Her eyes were full of water.

"Go fuck yourself." Anne dialled for a cab.

Matty stared at the fingers of his daughter's hand. The impossibly small nails. Fists like a boxer's. She sighed in her sleep. Her eyelids fluttered.

Lou had brought the vehicle out of a 360-degree spin and avoided the accident ahead of them by taking the shoulder. Matty figured after all those years of preaching, Lou had built up some credit with the Lord. But after that incident, he wasn't sure if there would be much left. Larry had reached forward from the back seat and patted the man on the shoulder. At least a minute elapsed before his father let go of the dash and sat back.

It took several days for Matty to bring his daughter home. Papers needed signing. The hospital required assurances. In the end, Anne cut through them like a buzz saw. His father hovered and hovered.

Larry spent most of his time in the lounge watching TV and drinking coffee. Or outside the front door smoking cigarettes. It took a great deal of coaxing before he'd take the baby, but once he had, he strutted around the hospital like a rooster. Couldn't put her down.

Old Vermaelen bought them a crib, and Lou set it up in Matty's room. Anne made more deliveries than Canada Post. Diapers, formula, burping towels, and clothes.

It was March break, but Matty couldn't imagine returning to school. Tomorrow was his birthday. He'd be eighteen. Nonetheless, Larry and Lou had already been hard at work on a schedule. He had only three months to graduation, they said. And then the worst was behind him.

Kim called him the first night he was back. Larry tried to hang up the phone, but eventually David wrestled it away.

"Is she beautiful?"

Matty was wary. "She's the most beautiful thing I've ever seen."

"We're just getting settled down here."

Matty allowed the silence to pour in.

She told him Taos was everything she'd hoped for. That the energy of the place was indescribable. She already had big plans for a series of paintings. Marc had begun to write. Eventually she tired of propping up the conversation.

"Matty?"

"What?"

"Did you choose a name?"

"We're going to call her Brooke."

Anne let herself in. The day was crisp and clear and cold. Inside, the house was warm and full of men. She was carrying a grocery bag, which Larry took from her. Only half of Vermaelen was visible under the sink, where he was fixing a leaky pipe. She had met him the day before. Lou had just arrived at the top of the cellar stairs. It was he who had driven her home from the hospital that first night to save her the cab fare. Her car was a writeoff, of course. Now she drove a big black SUV. In case she ran into Melanie again.

With the number of kilometres she had already clocked on it, driving back and forth to the house on Water Street, she would almost be better off to move.

"What's the prognosis?" David asked him.

"I think we'll begin holding our Thursday meetings here. It's going to take all hands. But she *will* ride again."

Matty stared up at his mother. "Hey."

Brooke was swaddled in the crook of his left arm. He held a bottle to her mouth with the other.

Larry circled in behind Matty and looked over his shoulder. "She sure has Henry in her by the way she takes to the bottle."

"Dad," David admonished.

The old man laughed until he coughed.

Vermaelen's voice rose out from under the sink, disembodied. "She's bald like you too."

"Just like Nat." David did not look up. "Do you remember, Anne?"

She held her breath, but no one else reacted. Feeling suddenly buoyant, she exhaled. "Yeah. She was almost a year old before she had anything at all.

"Do you remember how angry you were when she cut it?"

David scoffed, "Do I?"

He placed his finger by the baby's hand, and Brooke took it and held it there. The sound of her soft contented sucking broke through the commotion.

"Sit down, *Maman*." Matty nodded toward an empty chair. "Take your coat off and stay awhile."

Anne looked around at nothing in particular, and then held her own elbows. "No. I should really get back."

David lifted his head. "No, really. Please, sit down. We'll have someone deliver pizza."

"Nonsense," Lou cut in. "I will make us a perfectly good

spaghetti with this." He relieved Larry of the grocery bag and set it on the counter.

Anne nodded and let go of herself. She smiled at David, who smiled back and then looked down at Matty and his new granddaughter.

Matty would be eighteen in the morning, she thought. My god, where has the time gone.

The room was lit by the last light of the evening sun slanting in through the kitchen window above the sink. At that angle, it could not last longer than a few minutes. But while it did, everything was perfect.

And her eye was oh so quiet.

Acknowledgements

Thank you to my wife, Caroline. Thank you to Sharon Caseburg, Jamis Paulson, and Michelle Palansky at Turnstone. Thank you, most especially, to my editor, Michelle Berry, who made this a better book. And thank you to my daughter, Maija, for the title.

I consulted the informative website of The Merrickville Model Railroad Club during the writing of "The House on Water Street." Their organization is the inspiration behind the fictional Frontenac Model Railroad Club.